Retold Myths & Folktales

African Myths

African American Folktales

Asian Myths

Classic Myths, Volume 1

Classic Myths, Volume 2

Classic Myths, Volume 3

Mexican American Folktales

Native American Myths

Northern European Myths

World Myths

The Retold Tales® Series features novels, short story anthologies, and collections of myths and folktales.

Perfection Learning®

Contributing Writers

William S. E. Coleman, Jr.
M.A.T. English and Education
Educational Writer

Rebecca Spears Schwartz
M.A. English
Educational Writer

Retold Myths & Folktales

CLASSIC MYTHS

VOLUME 2

Perfection Learning®

Editor in Chief
Kathleen Myers

Inside Illustration
Tom Rosborough

Editors
Beth Obermiller
Rebecca Spears Schwartz

Book Design
Dea Marks

Cover Illustration
Greg Hargreaves

For information contact
Perfection Learning® Corporation
1000 North Second Avenue, P.O. Box 500
Logan, Iowa 51546-0500
Phone: 1-800-831-4190 • Fax: 1-800-543-2745
perfectionlearning.com

Paperback ISBN 0-8959-8994-8
Cover Craft® ISBN 0-8124-9147-5
19 20 21 22 PP 08 07 06 05 04

TABLE
OF CONTENTS

WELCOME TO THE RETOLD CLASSIC MYTHS

You see the references everywhere. Look at great artwork like the *Venus de Milo*. Or classic literature such as James Joyce's *Ulysses*. Then think about or language, which is filled with words like *typhoon and panic*. You can even see them in ads for FTD florist and Atlas moving company.

What do all these things, form art to ads, have in common? They're bases on Greek and Roman classic myths.

We call something classic when it is so well loved that it is saved and passed down to new generations. Classics have been around for a long time, but they're not dusty or out of date. That's because they are brought back to life by each new person who sees and enjoys them.

The Retold Classic Myths are stories written years ago that continue to entertain or influence today. The tales offer exciting plots, important themes, fascinating characters, and powerful language. They are stories that many people have loved to hear and share with one another.

RETOLD UPDATE

This book presents a collection of eight adapted classics. All the colorful, gripping, comic details of the older versions are here. But in the Retold versions of the stories, long sentences and paragraphs have been split up.

In addition, a word list had been added at the beginning of each story to make reading easier. Each word defined on that list is printed in dark type within the story. If you forget the meaning of a word while you're reading, just check the list to review the definition.

You'll also see footnotes at the bottom of some story pages. These notes identify people or places, explain ideas, show pronunciations, or even let you in on a joke.

We offer two other features you may wish to use. One is a two-part map of ancient Greece at the front of the book. The other is a list of the major gods, giving both their Greek and Roman names. You see, the Romans linked stories about their own gods to the Greek gods. So in many ways, the gods were identical. The list will help you keep all the names straight.

Finally, at the end of each tale you'll find some more information. These revealing and sometimes amusing facts will give you insight into ancient cultures, tellers of the myths, or related myths.

One last word. Since these myths have been retold so often, many versions exist. So a story you read here may differ from a version you read elsewhere.

Now on to the myths. Remember, when you read the Retold Tales, you bring each story back to life in today's world. We hope you'll discover why these tales have earned the right to be called classics.

MAPS OF ANCIENT GREECE

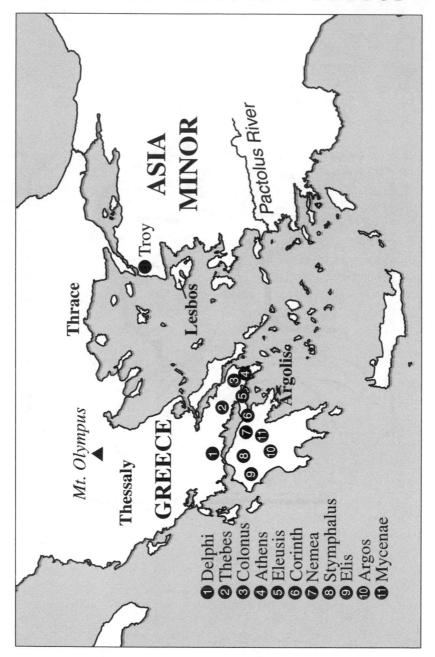

ASIA MINOR

Pactolus River

Troy

Thrace

Lesbos

Mt. Olympus

Thessaly

GREECE

Argolis

1 Delphi
2 Thebes
3 Colonus
4 Athens
5 Eleusis
6 Corinth
7 Nemea
8 Stymphalus
9 Elis
10 Argos
11 Mycenae

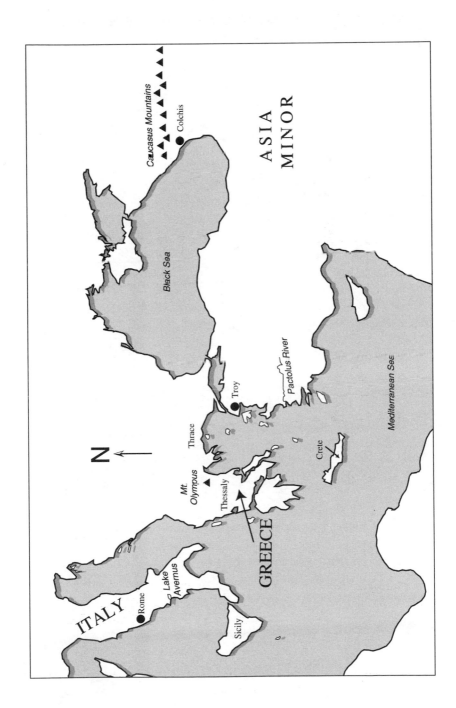

VOCABULARY PREVIEW

Below is a list of words that appear in the story. Read the
list and get to know the words before you start the story.

bittersweet—both painful and pleasant
blight—anything that ruins or destroys plant growth
blunt—plainspoken; not sensitive
chasm—opening in the earth; deep gap
contrary—opposite
deity—a divine being; a god
fasting—the act of going without food
haughty—proud; stuck-up
hospitable—friendly to guests
immortal—undying, living forever
nourishment—food
ominous—threatening; unlucky
pacify—to make peaceful or calm
perish—die
realm—a kingdom
reverence—deep respect; great admiration
rites—ceremonies; special religious acts
surged—poured; gushed
thrive—grow; blossom
yearning—a strong desire

The Theft of Persephone

Old age and death
have no power
over Greek gods.
Yet even the mightiest god
is the plaything of a
seemingly innocent force:
love.
And just as love can make
ordinary humans unhappy,
so it can tear a god in two.

The gods never weep. Or so it is said. But if they lose a loved one, do they grieve, even without tears? If so, how do they express their grief? And how does their grief affect the lives of humans?

Without doubt, the gods know the meaning of love. Aphrodite,[1] the goddess of love, always made sure of that. Human or god, it made no difference. No one was safe from her spell. Not even the cold god of the Underworld and ruler of the dead, mighty Hades.[2]

Hades' time came one day as he rode in his chariot around Sicily.[3] He drove wildly, calling his black horses by name.

Aphrodite caught sight of the **haughty** Hades. At once she called her son to her side.

"Eros,[4] take a look at that stubborn old rascal!" she exclaimed. "How unusual to see him riding here! And how lucky for us! To this day, he has refused to learn about love. But now we'll teach him. Go, child. Do your work."

Eros snatched up his bow and hurried away. He flew so fast, he managed to pass Hades. As he glided above the earth, he searched about.

Suddenly, in a nearby meadow, he spotted a young maiden picking flowers. Ah! Just what he was looking for. Here was the maiden to snare the heart of Hades!

The young maiden was actually the goddess Persephone.[5] Her mother was Demeter,[6] the goddess of the fields, who made all seeds grow. As much as she loved the earth, Demeter loved Persephone even more.

Eros smiled as he gazed at Persephone. She was such a lovely, flowerlike creature. Not surprisingly, she loved flowers more than anything in the world. In fact, she thought of little else. She spent days at a time picking them.

Eros readied his bow and arrow. Carefully he aimed it at a black dot on the horizon. The dot grew larger. Finally even a human eye could see it was the god Hades.

As Hades neared the meadow, Eros finally let loose his arrow. Faster than a hawk it flew through the air and struck

[1] (af rō dī´ tē)
[2] (hā´ dēz)
[3] (sis´ i lē) Sicily is an island off the southern coast of Italy.
[4] (er´ os   or ē´ ros)
[5] (per sef´ ō nē)
[6] (de mē´ ter)

its target. Eros smiled contentedly. Then with one look back, he turned towards home. His work was done.

Meanwhile, Eros' victim paused over the meadow and looked down. Hades was very puzzled. He had hardly felt the tiny sting of Eros' arrow. Yet as he gazed at Persephone, he felt a strange pain.

"What is this odd **yearning**?" he wondered. "Many young women have died and come to my kingdom. I felt nothing for them. Now why should my heart ache at the sight of this one?"

The troubled god drove on to Olympus to speak with his brother Zeus.[7] Zeus was the king of the gods and Persephone's father.

When he saw Hades approaching, Zeus shifted uneasily in his throne. "Not exactly a welcome guest," he thought to himself. "As much as I love my brother, his visits rarely lead to good."

But Hades was too wrapped up in his own problem to notice Zeus' reaction. He walked straight up to the throne and spoke. **Blunt** fellow that he was, he came right to the point.

"I want to marry your daughter Persephone. I have come to ask your permission."

Hades saw the flicker of surprise on his brother's face. "Yes, Zeus, love is strange to me. But after seeing Persephone, I have been conquered."

Zeus fidgeted. So he had been right about this visit after all.

"Dear brother," Zeus finally said, "nothing would please me more. But you know the girl's mother, Demeter. Persephone is her most beloved treasure. I can tell you right now that she'll have none of this.

"And think of the girl," Zeus continued. "Why, all she knows of life is sunlit fields. Can she possibly find happiness in your dark **realm**?"

[7](ō lim′ pus) (zūs)

But when Zeus saw Hades' sad expression, he paused. "Ah, brother, I know that look. Haven't I felt love's pain all too often?"

Zeus shook his head. At last he sighed. "Very well, she shall be yours. You're as good a husband as any."

At once the sadness lifted from Hades' face. Yet Zeus couldn't help but offer one last warning. "Be careful, brother. Her mother must not find out about this marriage."

So Hades set about planning to steal Persephone. For a number of days he watched the meadow closely. Finally he saw the lovely girl return.

As usual, Persephone had come to pick flowers. She wandered around the meadow, stooping here and there to pick a bloom. Then her eyes fell on a delightful blossom.

"Such colors!" she sighed. "And such a wonderful scent! Surely, this is the most beautiful flower I have ever seen!"

As Persephone bent to pick it, Hades sprang his trap. At once the earth opened up beneath Persephone's feet. She stepped back dizzily. The terrible **chasm** below was pitch black. Persephone had never imagined such darkness, even in her dreams.

As Persephone moved to escape, she heard a roar of wind and the clatter of hoofs. Suddenly she saw a chariot rushing up out of the darkness. In an instant, Hades had lifted her into the chariot.

Persephone was overcome with terror. She struggled fearfully. All the lovely flowers she had gathered scattered everywhere. The belt about her waist came undone and fell to the ground.

"Mother!" she cried. "Mother, help me! Oh, please help me!"

But Demeter couldn't hear her daughter's cries. Only the god Helios[8] witnessed the deed. As master of the sun, he drove his golden chariot across the sky each day. Now from high overhead, Helios watched the terrible scene. For a

[8](hē' li os)

moment, he considered coming to Persephone's rescue. But then he thought better of it.

"Poor girl," he said to himself. "The Underworld is no place for her. Still, it's best never to get mixed up in the business of one's fellow gods. Besides, I'm running late today as it is."

So without further trouble, Hades carried Persephone down to his kingdom. And there she was quickly crowned as his queen.

By evening, Demeter had noticed her daughter's absence. She went to the field where Persephone had been picking flowers. There she found Persephone's belt and the scattered flowers. But the chasm had sealed itself up. No hint remained of where Persephone had gone.

When Demeter saw these **ominous** signs, she nearly went mad. She ran wildly through the world, searching for her daughter. In grief, she tore at her clothes and called Persephone's name. But no answer came.

For nine days and nine nights Demeter searched. During all that time, she never slept nor ate. At night, she lit her way with two torches from the flames of a volcano.

At last, weary and starved, Demeter went to Helios.

"Sun-god, you see everything," she cried. "Whatever happened to my daughter, you must have witnessed it. Tell me! Out of pity, tell me! What happened to her?"

Helios decided it was best to tell the truth. "My poor woman," he said, "your daughter was carried off by Hades. She is now his queen in the Underworld."

"Do the other gods know of this?" asked Demeter.

"All, I'm afraid, except you," said Helios with sympathy.

"Then I have been betrayed. There is no one on earth or in heaven I can trust."

Demeter was stunned with grief and bitterness. She wandered the earth aimlessly. But no one recognized her as a great goddess. She went disguised as an elderly woman, dressed all in black.

At last, Demeter's travels brought her to Eleusis.[9] Every part of her ached—her bones, her heart, her spirit. Too weary to go on, she sat by the side of a stone well.

"I wish I were human," she said to herself. "If I were human, I could weep. If I were human, I could die."

While she sat there, four young sisters came to the well for water. They gazed curiously at Demeter. But she was too filled with grief to even notice them.

"You poor, sad woman," said the eldest, lifting the goddess' head. "What can we do to help you?"

"Leave me alone," moaned Demeter.

"But what terrible thing has happened to you?"

Demeter was not ready to reveal her identity. So she said, "I was captured by pirates. They planned to sell me as a slave. But I escaped and came here."

"Don't you have a place to stay?" asked the eldest sister.

"Don't let that worry you," said Demeter. "I can take care of myself. Besides, I can't trust you. I can't trust anyone. Even the gods hate me."

"But you don't understand," said the girl. "This is a very **hospitable** town. Any household would be glad to take you in. We'd be deeply pleased, though, if you'd agree to stay with us. Promise to stay here while we go ask our mother."

Too tired to quarrel, Demeter waited at the well. The girls returned before long, laughing with joy.

"Mother begs you to come at once!" they exclaimed. "She says you'll be our honored guest!"

And so Demeter followed the girls to their little home. They were met at the door by their mother, Metaneira.[10] She was the wife of a wise old man named Celeus.[11]

As Demeter stepped through the doorway, Metaneira stared at her. She sensed something special about the strange visitor.

---

[9] (e lū′ sis) Eleusis was a town in ancient Greece. As this story explains, it became known for its ceremonies honoring Demeter.

[10] (met a nī′ ra)

[11] (sē′ le us or sel′ e us)

"I don't know why," she whispered to her daughters, "but this sad old woman brings us great fortune."

Metaneira quickly moved a chair forward for Demeter. Then she offered the goddess some wine.

However, Demeter refused. "Bring me some mint-flavored water," she said. "That's all I want." This pleasant drink always made Demeter think of the farmers in her fields. It was what they liked to cool themselves with on hot summer days.

After drinking the water, Demeter rose from her chair. "And now I must leave," she said. "I do not wish to be a burden to you."

"Please, don't go," Metaneira begged with a kind smile. "You must stay and be the nurse to my son, Triptolemus."[12]

At once Metaneira fetched her newborn baby and brought it to Demeter. The goddess Demeter held the baby and looked into his eyes. Triptolemus laughed and gurgled and touched her face. For the first time since Persephone's disappearance, Demeter's heart swelled with joy.

"Yes," Demeter said at last. "Yes, I will stay."

And so Demeter devoted herself to Triptolemus' care. The sweet baby didn't make her forget her own lost daughter. To the **contrary**, she only thought of Persephone all the more. But for a time, the baby reminded her that life must go on in spite of her grief. And it reminded her of her love for all humans.

Yet a fear nagged at her. "What if I lose this precious boy, just as I lost Persephone?" she thought. "After all, he is human. Someday he must die—someday all too soon. Oh, no! That must not be! I couldn't bear it!"

So she decided to make the child **immortal**. That very night she began carrying out her plan. First, she fed the child ambrosia, the food of the gods. And when the household was asleep, she held the baby by the fireplace.

"Don't be afraid, little Triptolemus," she said tenderly. "These coals will burn away all that is human in you. Just

[12] (trip tol' e mus)

the god in you will be left. My only wish is to make you live forever.''

With those words, she set the baby in the burning coals.

Just as Demeter said, there was no cause to fear. The baby wasn't burned. Far from it. He smiled and giggled.

Night after night, Demeter fed the baby ambrosia and placed him in the coals. Triptolemus seemed to **thrive** on the treatment. He grew bigger and stronger by the hour.

Everyone in the family was delighted by the baby's progress. Everyone except his mother, Metaneira, that is. ''Somehow, I suspect this woman is practicing some strange magic,'' she thought.

One night, Metaneira didn't go to sleep at her usual time. Instead she hid and watched Demeter. She saw the goddess feed the baby ambrosia. Then came the frightening moment as Demeter moved towards the coals.

With a cry of alarm, Metaneira burst from her hiding place. She rushed forward and seized the child.

''How dare you!'' she cried. ''I trusted you with my baby! And now you want to murder him!''

Demeter rose to her feet in a rage. ''Foolish woman!'' she shouted. ''I would have made your child into a god! But now it cannot be.''

With those words, Demeter dropped her disguise. Gone was the dark-robed, sad old woman. The house was flooded with shining light. Metaneira stood face to face with a goddess.

''Truly, you are some **deity**!'' she wept. ''Who are you?''

''I am Demeter. I am the goddess of the earth, the grower of all seeds. **Nourishment** and life is what I offer you, not death. I feel nothing but love for humans like you. And what thanks do you give me in return?''

Metaneira fell to her knees. ''Forgive me, goddess!'' she cried. ''I did not know! But please, do not take my son's life because of my foolishness!''

Demeter's heart grew tender again. ''Poor woman,'' she said. ''Surely you don't think I would kill this boy? I love him more than any child I have ever known—except for my own lost daughter. He will grow to honor me. He will teach my ways to other humans.''

At that, Demeter wrapped herself in a cloud and disappeared.

The next day, a stunned Metaneira told her husband, Celeus, all that had happened. In turn, Celeus told the story to others. He also persuaded the townspeople to build a temple for Demeter.

The people worked long and hard on the temple. At last after many months, the beautiful building was finished. Then to their great joy, the townspeople learned that Demeter had returned to Eleusis. The temple had so pleased her that she made it her home.

But the goddess welcomed neither worshippers nor sacrifice. Still grieving for her daughter, she was determined to waste away forever.

The earth, too, suffered terribly. Demeter forgot her love for the land and allowed it to die. One month it rained too much. The next, it rained not at all. All crops, seeds, cattle, sheep, and goats began dying. People realized that before long, they would die as well. And all for Demeter's love of Persephone.

Persephone! What had become of her during this time? As Zeus had guessed, the girl so used to sunlight hated the gloomy Underworld. And she hated her husband for bringing her there.

Hades sensed this and tried to **pacify** her with rare jewels. But these gifts did not please Persephone. Instead, she threw them angrily away.

"Why do you bring these ugly stone flowers to me?" she cried.

"Because no flowers grow here," replied her husband.

"I want living things near me or nothing at all."

Yet Hades kept bringing her jewels. In time, Persephone actually came to admire their cold beauty. They seemed to reflect her own sadness.

Queenhood grew on the young goddess as well. She wandered among the dead, sharing their memories of life in the sun. She also learned to share their sadness.

Truly, life in the Underworld deeply changed Persephone. Before going there, she cared for nothing but flowers. In Hades, she learned to care for human souls. And so Persephone grew to womanhood.

The goddess even learned to care for her husband a little. But she didn't dare tell or show him that. If she did, she knew there was no hope of ever seeing the sun again. So Persephone never looked upon her husband except with a frown. And she refused ever to eat.

Meanwhile, the horrible **blight** went on for a year. Finally Zeus knew that he must step in if humans were to survive. So he sent Hermes,[13] the messenger god, to Demeter's temple with a summons.

When Demeter heard the summons, she spoke harshly to Hermes. "Take this message to the king of the gods. If he wants to speak with me, he must come here himself. And he must come here with my daughter. Then—and only then—will the earth live again."

Hermes returned with Demeter's message. Zeus listened in grim silence. Then he called all the other gods except Hades before his throne.

"Fellow deities," he said, "you know the dreadful thing that has happened. Demeter has forgotten the earth. Humankind itself will soon **perish**. I needn't tell you how terrible this will be for us. No more temples will be built in our honor. No more musicians will sing our praises. No more poets will tell of our adventures.

"But worst of all," he continued, "no sacrifices will be offered up to us. We will be immortal always. Yet our reason for immortality will be gone!"

Of course, this speech caused quite a stir. Zeus waited until the gods' angry voices died down. Then he said, "Demeter must be made to change her mind. It was I, I'm

[13] (her' mēz)

afraid, who brought on her anger. She'll hear nothing from me. Only you can pacify her.''

So, one by one, the gods of Olympus visited Demeter in her temple. They brought her beautiful gifts. Each begged her to be kind to the earth again. But, one by one, she turned them away—all except the last one, Hermes.

To him she said, "Tell Zeus that I shall come and speak with him. But tell him also that my heart hasn't changed. Only the return of my daughter will restore life to the earth."

Hermes delivered the message. And before long, Demeter left her temple and returned to Olympus.

Zeus met Demeter at his throne. "Sister,"[14] he said, "heartlessness does not become you. You must remember your love for humankind."

"And you must remember what I have said," replied Demeter. "Unless my daughter is returned to me, nothing on earth shall live."

"I can imagine how you feel," said Zeus.

"You have no idea how I feel," Demeter coldly replied.

"But be reasonable! You have no cause to disapprove of this marriage. Hades is one of the greatest of all the gods. In his own realm, he's as powerful as I am."

"In his own realm!" cried Demeter. "In the realm of darkness, you mean! In the realm of the dead!"

"And whom would you prefer to be her husband?" snapped Zeus. "Your daughter is a queen in the Underworld! Can you wish anything better for her?"

But then sensing her pain, Zeus spoke more soothingly. "Come now, Demeter. All parents must give up their children sooner or later. Bear this loss gracefully."

"I will bear nothing gracefully," answered Demeter. "The entire universe will know my grief forever. Only one thing can change that. And you know what it is."

"Then I see I have no choice," Zeus said. "I shall send for your daughter at once. But understand one thing.

---

[14] Demeter was Zeus' sister and, at one time, his wife. (As the story mentions, Persephone is their child.)

Persephone cannot return to you if she has eaten anything in Hades' realm. This is not my decision but that of the Fates[15] themselves. Nothing can change it.''

''I have no reason to worry,'' said Demeter. ''My daughter could never be happy in the Underworld. I know that she has wasted away there. Just as I have here.''

Demeter returned to her temple to wait. And Zeus sent Hermes to fetch Persephone.

When Persephone heard Hermes' news, she was delighted. Oh, to see the sun again! But then she noticed her husband's heartbroken face. Pity for him **surged** in her heart. Still, she was careful not to show it.

As for Hades, his heart was torn. ''I love her dearly,'' he thought. ''How can I give her up? And yet, the poor girl is so unhappy here. And I cannot wish a life of sadness for her. What can I do?''

Guiltily, Hades realized he could not let Persephone go. But how could he keep her? Then he remembered what the Fates had said . . .

When the moment came to leave, Hades took Persephone by the hand.

''It is well that we part,'' he said. ''You have found no joy in my realm. Still, there is one memory I would like us to share.''

Hades held a pomegranate[16] in his hand and broke it open.

Then he said to Persephone, ''To this day, you have eaten nothing in the Underworld. You have not allowed yourself one moment of joy. But now please share one happy moment with me. Let us both remember this little meal.''

Persephone was touched. The pomegranate, after all, was a symbol of marriage. And she had been the wife of Hades, if just for a short while. Her wish was only to see flowering fields again, not to leave Hades unhappy.

''I've shown this lonely god nothing but coldness,'' she thought. ''But now I know that I'm leaving. What harm

---

[15] The Fates were goddesses who decided the future of men and women. In some versions of the myths, even Zeus is forced to accept their judgments.

[16] A pomegranate is a large, thick-skinned fruit filled with seeds.

can it do to show him a bit of kindness?"

And so Persephone tasted the pomegranate. Its seeds were sweet and welcome after a long year of **fasting**.

The meal at an end, Hades brought forth his chariot. Then he and his wife headed for the land of sun.

When Persephone reached her mother's temple, the two of them rushed to embrace.

"Oh, let me look at you!" said Persephone.

"And let me look at you!" exclaimed Demeter.

Demeter was a little surprised at what she saw. This Persephone was almost a stranger. The girl had a new look in her eyes. In fact, she was not a girl at all but a wise and gentle woman.

Most of all, Demeter was disturbed that Persephone did not look thin and hungry. The little pomegranate had given her great nourishment.

"Can she have eaten something in the Underworld?" worried Demeter. "Oh, no. I can't even think of that."

And so the two of them talked and talked. Demeter told of her grief and her travels. And she praised the kindness of the people in Eleusis. Persephone, in her turn, spoke of life in the Underworld. She told both the good and the bad.

"He is a good man in his way," she confessed. "A fine husband, too—though not for me. But I did him one small kindness before I left. I shared a pomegranate with him."

Poor Demeter's face went white. She wanted to scream, but her throat was closed and dry.

"Mother!" cried Persephone. "What's wrong? What have I done?"

"I've lost you, my child," gasped Demeter. "I've lost you forever."

The earth, which had just begun to grow, began to wilt and shrivel again.

"Mother, tell me!" begged Persephone.

"The pomegranate!" wailed Demeter. "The pomegranate!"

But at that moment, they found themselves surrounded

by a strange light. They turned and saw that another goddess was present. It was Rhea,[17] Demeter's mother, the oldest of gods. She stood before them, shining with wisdom.

"Do not grieve, Demeter," said Rhea. "Nor you, Persephone. My son Zeus has sent me with good news. Persephone shall spend only one-third of each year in the Underworld. The other two-thirds she shall spend above the earth."

The news was **bittersweet**. But mother and daughter embraced happily. Now they would not have to be separated forever.

And so for the next eight months, Persephone lived in the sunlight. During this time, Demeter allowed the earth to live and grow again. Crops and animals grew strong and healthy. Humankind was no longer in danger.

And Persephone roamed her fields again. But she no longer picked her beloved flowers. Instead, she looked upon them with love and **reverence**. She now knew that no earthly thing lives forever.

When her time on earth was over, Persephone went to the Underworld. During those four months, Demeter fell sad again. Once more she let the earth grow cold and lifeless. But with Persephone's return came spring.

Throughout the year, Demeter remained at her temple in Eleusis. She taught Metaneira's boy, Triptolemus, to be her priest. Each year at Persephone's return, he led the people of Eleusis in celebration. These were Demeter's holy "mysteries." Only humans chosen by Demeter knew the **rites**. So the goddess honored the townfolk and they honored her.

The story of Demeter and Persephone explains how the seasons came to be. But the story tells much more than that. It also reveals the seasons of the heart, the cycle of happiness and sadness. Both come to us time and time again.

To love is to grieve, and all gods and humans must do both. That is because the goddess Demeter lives in each of us.

[17] (rē′ a)

INSIGHTS

Demeter taught Triptolemus all the secrets of agriculture. She gave him the first seed of corn. She also showed him how to use oxen to plow. And she taught him how to plant a field with grain.

In turn, Triptolemus spread this knowledge all over the world. His travels were made easier by a gift from Demeter: a chariot pulled by two dragons.

From the Roman name for Demeter—which is *Ceres*—comes the word *cereal*. The reason is obvious since the goddess was in charge of agriculture, especially grain.

The religious rituals begun at Eleusis were very special to the Greeks. They were so special that the Greeks observed them for 2,000 years.

Parts of the ritual were surrounded in great mystery. (They are actually called the Eleusinian Mysteries.) But from what is known and can be guessed, they involved fasting and prayer. There was a more joyous side, too, as people paraded and danced.

The holiest moments of the rituals included a staging of Demeter's story. Then at the climax of the event, an ear of grain would be shown. Of course, this grain symbolized the goddess herself.

Perhaps the rituals don't seem so mysterious now. But those who watched the more private rituals swore on pain of death to keep them secret.

continued

The Greeks believed that almost all humans ended up in the Underworld. True, a few rare souls—such as Heracles—were asked to join the gods on Olympus. But everyone else died and became Hades' subjects.

Thus most Greeks respected and feared Hades. In fact, they invented other names for him to avoid using the word "Hades." They called him Pluto, or "giver of plenty," and Dis, or "the wealthy one." Sometimes they didn't even use a name at all, just polite titles. This was believed to be safer than speaking of him directly.

Even the worship of Hades was performed with caution. At the moment when an animal—usually a black sheep—was sacrificed to him, people turned away their heads.

Not that many sacrifices were performed anyway. The terrifying Hades had few altars.

Pigs are strangely linked with Demeter and Persephone. Some myths say that Demeter couldn't trace her daughter because pigs had trampled over Persephone's footprints. These same pigs fell into the chasm created when Hades split the earth.

In later worship of Demeter, pigs were thrown into a pit. Figures of wheat and flour were also tossed in. These strange sacrifices were meant to stand for the pigs and humans of the original story.

ODYSSEUS AND THE CYCLOPS

VOCABULARY PREVIEW

Below is a list of words that appear in the story. Read the list and get to know the words before you start the story.

civilized—refined; cultured
contemplated—thought about; considered
cowered—crouched in fear
dazed—stunned; confused
defiled—made dirty or unclean; polluted
deserts—(an) earned reward or punishment
exquisite—fine; excellent
groped—blindly searched
hospitality—friendly treatment of guests
mocked—made fun of; scorned
natives—lifelong residents
pathetically—pitifully
potent—powerful
rocked—shook; trembled
scoundrel—bad person; rascal
sinister—threatening; evil
slaughtered—brutally murdered; butchered
sneered—smirked; snickered
sowing—planting
vital—very important; necessary

ODYSSEUS
and the
CYCLOPS

from *THE ODYSSEY*

Can a man be clever enough to outwit the most dangerous foe? Can a man be so clever that he outwits even himself? Judge for yourself in this story of the cleverest of all Greek heroes.

Have the gods forgotten me?'' Odysseus[1] wondered. He had been sailing with his twelve ships for days now. A storm had separated them from the rest of the Greek fleet. And now they were lost—hopelessly lost.

[1](ō dis′ ūs or ō dis′ sē us)

The Trojan[2] War was over, after ten years of bloody struggle. The Greeks had won a great but hard-earned victory. Odysseus had fought bravely and well. And he had looked forward to the journey home.

But some of the Greeks had gone crazy with the victory. They had **defiled** the temple of the goddess Athena in Troy.[3] Athena had supported the Greeks throughout the war, but this act made her wild with rage. She turned against the Greeks and plotted to destroy them. On their return voyage, she made sure they met a terrible storm.

Poor Odysseus was not really to blame for the temple's destruction. He had always been a religious man, favored by the gods. But now all he could do was wonder: "Have the gods forgotten me?"

It seemed as though they had. When the storm clouds cleared, Odysseus realized they were lost. Though they spotted land, it wasn't home. Yet at least the weary travelers hoped to find food and fresh water.

The ships landed, and Odysseus sent three men to explore. "Find out who lives here," he commanded. "Make friends with them. Tell them we need food and drink."

The men did as they were told. They hadn't traveled far before they met the **natives**. They were peaceful, gentle people. They offered the sailors flowers to eat.

"What kind of flower is this?" asked Odysseus' men.

"The lotus," explained the natives. "They're all the food you'll ever need."

Odysseus' men ate the lotus. The sweet taste immediately delighted them.

Then a more **sinister** change began to occur. Their eyes glazed over. Their motions became lazy—almost dreamlike.

Slowly they made their way back to their ships. In their hands, they carried more lotus blossoms.

"Try some of these berries, Odysseus!" they called. They grinned from ear to ear. "You'll never long for home again!"

[2](trō' jan)
[3](a thē' na) (troi)

Odysseus angrily knocked the blossoms from their hands. "Get back on board," he commanded. "We sail at once."

The three men hung back, gazing stupidly at their angry commander.

"Go? 'Go,' he says," **mocked** the first man. "And why should we? What do you offer us except rough seas and hard rowing? What chance do we have of ever getting home again? Why, the gods themselves have given us up!"

"And what if we do get home?" asked the second man in a sleepy voice. "What then? Our wives have forgotten us and taken new husbands. Our children have grown up not knowing us. They are happy without us. And we can be happy here!"

"These Lotus-Eaters are savages," barked Odysseus. "Do you want to be like them, lazy and useless? We are **civilized** men. And civilization takes sweat and hard work."

"Well, if they are savages, they are happier for it," laughed the third man.

But Odysseus wouldn't hear their plea. He hauled them back on ship by force and tied them to the ship's benches. They begged and pleaded. But Odysseus closed his ears.

Then he waved to the rest of his men. "Come aboard!" he shouted. "And whatever you do, don't eat any of that lotus plant!"

Reluctantly the rest of the crew returned and settled behind the oars.

As the ships sailed away, Odysseus considered his situation. "So far from home," he thought. "And so little hope of return! Were those three **dazed** fools right? Have we truly been forgotten by those who love us? Would it have been better to stay and join the Lotus-Eaters?"

Odysseus thought of his home, the island of Ithaca.[4] He also thought of his wife, Penelope, and his son, Telemachus.[5] It had been ten years since he had seen them. Telemachus must be a young man by now. And Penelope—

4 (ith' a ka)
5 (pe nel' ō pē) (te lem' a kus)

could she have taken another husband? Could they have forgotten him?

But then he seemed to see Penelope waiting for him with open arms. Odysseus' heart filled with hope.

"What a fool I am to worry!" he thought with a rush of relief. "I know my dear Penelope has waited for me. And she always will for as long as any hope remains. As for my son, he is fine, strong, and eager to meet his father."

Just as night was about to fall, they sighted land again. More careful this time, Odysseus landed his ships on a near-by island.

It was night now. Yet with the moonlight as their guide, the crew quickly explored the island. They found it to be a rough wilderness. Short, twisted trees grew between grassy patches. Small streams of water dashed between rocks. And wild goats roamed everywhere.

Odysseus' men killed a few of the goats and sat down to a feast. As they ate, one man commented, "Surely, no one lives on the mainland. Otherwise, they would have farmed this island. They would have tamed these goats."

But Odysseus pointed to the mainland. As they stared, they spotted what their sharp-eyed leader had seen. The smoke from dozens of fires was rising into the dim moonlight.

"Someone lives there," he said. "And tomorrow we'll find out who."

At dawn, Odysseus ordered eleven of the ships to remain on the island. Then with only one ship, he set sail for the mainland.

Upon landing, Odysseus split the group. Half would guard the ship and half would explore. He himself set off at once with the exploring party.

They found the country was a tangled wilderness. Wheat, barley, and vines thick with grapes grew wild everywhere. They had to cut their way through the brush.

"What kind of people would let their crops grow like this?" asked one of the men. "Don't they know anything of **sowing** or plowing?"

"Savages," said Odysseus, fighting his way through the growth. "But savages of a different kind than the Lotus-Eaters. See there? Up on that mountain?"

Odysseus pointed to a cave high above them. The huge opening was surrounded by a great stone fence.

"These people live with their animals in caves like that. They probably know nothing of poetry or music. Or government and friendship. They may not even know each other's names."

He **contemplated** the cave for a minute. "Still, we'll pay that cave a visit. And we'll take some wine along to show our good will. If they're savages, let's hope they're friendly at least."

They climbed the slope to the cave and cautiously walked inside. There they found a few lambs penned up. They also saw enormous baskets of cheese scattered around.

The men darted forward at once to grab hunks of the cheese. Hungrily they bit into the rich food.

"Let's pack away as much of this cheese as we can," said one of Odysseus' men. "And then let's get out of here at once."

"A fine idea," said another. "I don't look forward to meeting the brute who lives here."

But Odysseus only laughed. "Is that any way to thank our host for his fine cheese? Brute though he may be, we must stay and meet him."

Odysseus regretted his words almost at once, for a huge shadow suddenly darkened the cave. Odysseus and his men whirled. There in the doorway stood a gigantic monster. He had but one eye in the center of his forehead. A Cyclops![6]

The giant didn't see them at first. He was busy herding his flock of sheep into the cave. So the terrified humans had time to hide themselves.

As they **cowered** in various corners, the Greeks fearfully watched the Cyclops. They saw him pick up a huge boulder

[6] (sī′ klops)

with amazing ease. Then with a grunt, he shut the mouth of the cave behind him. Next he sat down and began to milk his goats and sheep.

Finally, with his milking finished, the Cyclops started a fire. As the flames flickered through the cave, the Cyclops at last saw the huddled men.

"Who's there!" he called out in a thunderous voice. His one eye darted to and fro. "Are you pirates who've come to steal? Or are you traders who've come to buy and sell? In either case, you're unwelcome."

Though terror shook him, Odysseus bravely stepped forward. "Neither pirates nor traders," he said as calmly as possible. "Just weary warriors, on our way home. All we ask is your **hospitality**. A little food and water—whatever you can spare. If you respect the gods, you'll treat us well. Zeus[7] always smiles down on a kind host."

The Cyclops threw his head back and laughed horribly. "Zeus! You little fool! You dare talk to me of Zeus! Why, I'm stronger than Zeus or any other god. None of them can stop me from doing whatever I like with you!" He gave another fierce laugh.

Suddenly he gave Odysseus a cunning look with his fierce eye. "But tell me something, little man, and maybe I won't hurt you. Where did you land your ship? Nearby or far away?"

Odysseus was too smart to fall for that trick. "Our ship was destroyed in a storm," he lied. "We clung to bits of wreckage. Many of our number drowned. These men and I barely made it to your shore alive."

Odysseus stood trembling for a moment. He wondered if the Cyclops believed him.

"That may be the last mistake you ever make," the giant chuckled. With a lunge, he grabbed two of the men. Raising them high in the air, he dashed their brains out on the rocks.

The others watched in horror as the Cyclops cut his two

---

[7](zūs) Zeus was the king of the gods and the ruler of the heavens.

victims limb from limb. Then with dreadful smacking sounds, he ate them greedily. Finally, quite happy with his awful meal, the Cyclops went to sleep.

The Greeks huddled in a corner of the cave, moaning with fear. They were truly trapped. All of them together could not move that boulder. They were forced to sit shaking in the dark through the long night.

Odysseus prayed hard while he waited. "Almighty Zeus, please help me," he pleaded. "Or if you have no help to give, just tell me what to do!"

No reply came. Odysseus was disappointed but not too surprised. In days gone by, the gods replied more willingly. Even the greatest heroes seldom relied on their wits alone. They simply asked some god for help or advice. And the gods often spoke to them.

Now, however, the heavens were often silent. "The gods seem to speak to us less and less these days," grumbled Odysseus. "Perhaps that's what comes from being civilized."

Yet though he complained, Odysseus was used to think ing for himself. Normally, he enjoyed the challenge. Now, however, he would have liked some help.

Odysseus scratched his beard thoughtfully. "It will take some brains to get us out of this mess," he muttered.

Odysseus studied the Cyclops while he slept. It would be easy for Odysseus to stab him with a sword. But that would be just a pinprick to this monster. He'd have to think of something else.

The next morning, the Cyclops arose. He milked his flock, then had his breakfast: two more of Odysseus' men. As he ate, he grinned and rubbed his belly with satisfaction.

"Time to leave you, little men," he rumbled. "But don't feel *you* must leave. In fact, I won't hear of it. After all, Zeus is always kind to those who are hospitable."

With an evil roar of laughter, the giant herded his flocks out of the cave. Outside, he paused and rolled the boulder back to the entrance. Once again Odysseus and his men were sealed in.

They sat all day and wondered what to do.

"An awful fix this is!" cried one of the men. "Farmed and **slaughtered** like the animals around us! He'll kill us two by two, until there are none of us left!"

"Not if I can help it," declared Odysseus. "I have an idea. It may not work, but we must try."

He pointed to the shepherd's staff which the Cyclops had left behind. This staff was a huge tree trunk, as long as a ship's mast.

Odysseus instructed his men to cut six feet off the end. Then Odysseus carved the pole to a sharp point. He burned the point in the fire to make it harder.

"But what are we going to do with this great stick of yours?" asked one of Odysseus' men.

"We're going to shove it into the Cyclops' eye," said Odysseus.

The men raised cries of protest.

"But that's impossible!" cried one.

"How can we even get near enough to him?" exclaimed another.

"Leave that to me," said Odysseus. "But I'll need four men to help me carry this pole."

The crew drew straws. Odysseus was pleased that the four strongest men were chosen.

When evening came, the Cyclops returned. Once again, he herded his flock inside and sealed the entrance. Then he milked his sheep, gobbled two more men, and built up the fire.

Now was the time to act. Odysseus brought out the wine he had carried along. It was delicious wine—and **potent**. Odysseus usually mixed it with twenty parts of water before drinking it. But now he poured it straight into a cup. Then taking a deep breath, he stepped forward.

"Most excellent monster," he said, "I hope you enjoyed your meal."

The Cyclops belched contentedly.

"Here," said Odysseus, holding out the cup. "Have some of this fine Greek wine to wash my friends down. I meant to give it to you when we first met. But you behaved so badly, I kept it to myself. Drink it now. Perhaps you'll like it enough to let us go."

"Most hospitable of you," **sneered** the Cyclops. He snatched the cup away from Odysseus and drank greedily. A slow smile crossed the giant's face.

"Well!" exclaimed the Cyclops. "This is an excellent drink indeed! I make fine wine from my own grapes. But I must admit, your wine is even better! Give me more of it!" And the Cyclops shoved the cup in Odysseus' face.

"Oh, but I had hoped to save some for my companions," said Odysseus.

"Come, come," said the Cyclops, "there's not that many of you left!" He laughed heartlessly. Then he stared more curiously at Odysseus. "So where do you and your fine wine come from, little man? Now that I think of it, I don't even know your name. Mine is Polyphemus.[8] What's yours?"

Odysseus remained silent.

"Well, whoever you are," said the Cyclops, "*please* let me have some more of your wine. I'll give you a fine gift in return."

"Do you swear by the River Styx?"[9] asked Odysseus.

Polyphemus grunted. "By the River Styx, I swear it!"

So Odysseus poured another cup for the monster—and then another and another. The Cyclops began to sway drunkenly. His single eye drooped and grew foggy.

Odysseus saw his chance. "Good Polyphemus," he said. "It seems that you're enjoying my **exquisite** wine."

The Cyclops nodded stupidly.

"You asked my name," said Odysseus. "Since we're good drinking companions, I feel safe in telling you. My name

[8](pol i fē' mus)

[9](stiks) The gods swore by the River Styx when making a promise. This river flowed through Hades, the Underworld.

is Noman."[10] He paused and cunningly watched the giant. "Well, since we've been properly introduced, what about that gift you promised?"

The monster began to chuckle horribly. "Noman, eh? A fine name for dessert! I'll tell you what your gift will be. I'll eat all your friends before I eat you. You'll be the last to die."

Quite pleased with his joke, Polyphemus rolled over on his side. He was soon fast asleep. Wine dripped from his mouth. His snoring echoed through the cave.

Odysseus quickly motioned for the four chosen men to come forward. Together, they grabbed the pole and shoved it into the hot ashes of the fire. There they held it until it was white hot.

"It's ready," Odysseus whispered. "Now back up and take your places. Ready? Forward! Straight for his eye!"

With a mighty rush, the men charged towards the Cyclops and thrust the blazing point into his eye.

Drunk though he was, Polyphemus felt that pain! He sat up with a roar that shook the walls of the cave. In one quick motion, he'd seized the burning post and yanked it out of his eye. Still he roared.

Those screams **rocked** the cave. And they were also heard by every Cyclops in the area. Though not exactly neighborly, they came running to Polyphemus' cave.

"What's the matter with you, Polyphemus?" asked his closest neighbor. He rapped on the boulder blocking the entrance. "Why are you waking us up at this time of night? Is someone trying to kill you?"

"It's Noman!" wailed Polyphemus. "Noman is killing me!"

"Well then, if no man is killing you, why kick up such a fuss? If you're sick, don't expect us to help you. Say your prayers to your father Poseidon.[11] Now go back to bed and

---

[10] (nō′ man)

[11] (pō sī′ don) Poseidon was the god of the sea and bringer of earthquakes. He was also Polyphemus' father.

keep quiet. Let the rest of us sleep.''

Odysseus could hardly keep from laughing aloud. But silence was **vital** at this point. He and his men scarcely dared to breathe as Polyphemus staggered about, trying to find them.

At last the giant went to the entrance of the cave and **groped** for the boulder. With a shout of rage, he pushed it away from the mouth of the cave. Then he sat squarely in the middle of the entrance. He stretched out his arms so that no one could pass by unnoticed.

"What an old fool!" whispered Odysseus to his nearest companion. "Does he really think we'll try to just walk out?"

"And what else do you suggest?" hissed his companion.

Odysseus abruptly realized that he had no idea. He briefly considered a quick prayer to Zeus. But there was no time for that. He had to think fast.

The bleating of a fat sheep gave Odysseus an idea. With a glance around the cave, he found what he was looking for. As cautiously as possible, he tiptoed over to the Cyclops' bed. It was made of slender, flexible twigs.

Busily, Odysseus removed some of those twigs. Then he braided them together into lengths of rope. Next he gathered some of the rams together and roped them into groups of three.

Finally he beckoned to his men. "I'm going to tie you beneath these rams." His voice was the softest of whispers. "That way you can escape the cave in the morning when Old No-Eyes lets out his sheep. He shouldn't be able to find you if you stay beneath the middle ram."

Odysseus carried out his plan. But with everyone else safely tied, there was no one to help him. So he climbed beneath the biggest, finest ram and clung to the wool for dear life. He and his men stayed under the rams all night long.

Dawn came. The rams began to wander out of the cave. Polyphemus fingered their wool, searching for the men. Each group of three rams passed, one by one. Polyphemus groaned in pain and misery, failing to find a single man.

At last, the great ram carrying Odysseus came to the entrance. Polyphemus stopped the ram and touched him.

"Ah, my faithful old fellow," he cried **pathetically**. "You're always the first out of the cave. But not today! What's the matter? Perhaps it's pity for your master's eye that slows you. Oh, how I wish you could talk! You'd tell me where that rascal Noman is hiding! But I'll find him yet! I'll find him and smash his head in!"

Finally Polyphemus let the ram pass, with Odysseus underneath. Odysseus waited until he got a good distance from the cave. Then he dropped off the ram and freed his companions. Together, they chased the beasts down to the ship.

The men who had stayed to guard the ship were delighted to see their lost companions again. But upon hearing the fate of the missing, they wept and cursed.

"There will be time for tears and oaths later!" barked Odysseus. "Get as many of these beasts on board as you can. We're shoving off!"

The men rowed like fury. Before they were very far away, Odysseus shouted to the Cyclops.

"Hello, most excellent monster!" he yelled. "Your dessert got away, did he? Ah, well, that's your just **deserts**, you might say! That's what you get for being a poor host who eats his guests! That's what you get for mocking Zeus!"

At the sound of Odysseus' voice, Polyphemus came charging out of his cave. "Noman!" he screamed. "This is what you get for mocking *me!*" He picked up a boulder as big as the ship. Then he threw it violently into the sea.

The huge stone crashed into the water just ahead of the ship. It raised a great wave which swept the ship backward. Before they knew it, Odysseus and his companions were beached again.

The men quickly picked up poles and pushed their ship away from the shore. "Row if you love your lives!" Odysseus shouted to the men. And row they did.

Odysseus waited until they were twice as far from the shore as before. Then he shouted again, "Thinking of revenge, Polyphemus? Want to kill me, do you?"

One of Odysseus' shipmates angrily grabbed him. "Odysseus, you fool!" he exclaimed. "You got us out of danger with your cleverness. Will you kill us now through your stupidity?"

But Odysseus shoved the man away and kept shouting to the shore. "Maybe our paths will cross again some day! In that case, you'll want to know my name. And no, it's not Noman. I am Odysseus, the conqueror of Troy.[12] And I live in Ithaca. One day soon, if Zeus is willing, you can find me there!"

A great cry of misery rose up from the island. "Then it was true! A wise man once warned me of this! He said I would be defeated by a man named Odysseus! But I didn't expect it would be you. You seemed so small and weak. I expected a giant like myself— only stronger."

Polyphemus groaned again in rage and pain. "Come back to me again, Odysseus!" he wailed. "I've learned my lesson! This time I'll be kind to you! And this time, I have a real gift to offer! I'll pray to my father Poseidon to give you a safe journey! Maybe he'll cure my eye as well!"

Odysseus sneered. "No one will ever give you back your eye! I'm sure of that! I only wish I were as sure of your death!"

An awful silence followed. Then the men heard the giant praying to Poseidon.

"My father, lord of all the seas! Make sure this **scoundrel** never reaches his native land again! Or if he must, make sure it is only after long suffering and unhappiness!"

Then Polyphemus picked up one more huge rock and hurled it into the sea. This one fell just short of the ship.

---

[12] Odysseus came up with the plan for the Trojan Horse. The Greek army followed his suggestion and built a huge, hollow, wooden horse. Then they hid in the horse and were towed inside Troy. At night, they emerged and conquered the city.

It raised another great wave, which pushed the ship forward to the island.

There Odysseus met his waiting companions and their eleven ships. They had all been deeply worried and felt greatly relieved to see the survivors. But they also grieved for those who had died.

The men divided up the rams evenly among all the ships. All the sailors agreed that Odysseus should keep his great ram.

But Odysseus didn't plan to keep the beast for himself. While the others feasted into the night, Odysseus led his ram away. On a lonely hill, he sacrificed it to Zeus.

As he finished, Odysseus raised up this prayer: "Lord Zeus, king of the heavens, I did a foolish thing today. I taunted Polyphemus, the son of your brother Poseidon. And he brought down a terrible curse on me. It was wrong to do, and I regret it. Can you help me? Can you save me?"

But no answer came from the god.

The next day Odysseus set sail with his men, more unsure than ever.

He had every reason to worry, for Poseidon had heard his son's prayer. Odysseus and his men were no longer forgotten by the gods. Soon—very soon—they would wish they had been.

INSIGHTS

Odysseus is a rare hero in Greek myths. He was much more famous for his wisdom than his muscles. That wisdom won him respect—and sometimes jealousy. After the great warrior Achilles was slain in battle, Odysseus and another Greek rescued his body. This second Greek, Ajax, was known for his bravery and strength.

As a reward for their mission, both Greeks hoped to receive Achilles' armor. It was left to Thetis, Achilles' mother, to decide which hero was more deserving. She chose Odysseus, thus placing wisdom before strength. Afterward, Ajax went mad and then killed himself out of shame.

Odysseus was definitely not the battle-hungry type. In fact, he wanted to avoid going to the Trojan War altogether. Therefore, he decided to pretend he was mad. Yoking the odd team of an ass and ox to his plow, he began to plant salt.

But, Palamedes, the Greek who was sent to recruit Odysseus, suspected trickery. So he placed Odysseus' young son Telemachus in the path of the plow. Odysseus turned away, showing that he was no madman.

It's unfortunate for Odysseus that his trick with the plow didn't work. For he spent ten long years fighting in the Trojan War. Then his difficult journey home took another ten years. Thus his name gave birth to the word *odyssey,* which means a long adventure or quest.

continued

Cyclops stems from Greek words meaning *circle* and *eye*. This same root word is present in *encyclopedia*—a reference for "circular" or complete learning. Perhaps more appropriately, Cyclops is also linked with *cyclone*. This storm has a low-pressure center which causes air to flow in a circle. And like Odysseus' Cyclops, it can be very violent.

Little is actually known about Homer, supposed author of both *The Iliad* and *The Odyssey*. Some scholars believe he was blind. Some believe he was actually two separate men. Others don't believe he lived at all.

Whatever the facts might be, it is known that the Greeks based their religious views on Homer's portrayals of the gods. They also copied his characters and plots in many of their own dramas. They even used Homer's works as basic textbooks in their schools.

ACHILLES AND HECTOR

VOCABULARY PREVIEW

Below is a list of words that appear in the story. Read the list and get to know the words before you start the story.

anguish—great sorrow; agony
avenged—revenged
barbarian—one who is not civilized; a savage
carnage—slaughter; massacre
comrades—people who serve or work together
deprive—take away from; withhold or deny
donned—put on; dressed
exulting—rejoicing greatly
gloated—bragged
grudgingly—not willingly
invulnerable—can't be hurt; unconquerable
lure—tempt; persuade
masquerading—disguising; wearing a costume
meddling—interfering; butting in
mutilated—torn limb from limb; badly scarred
prophecy—prediction; fortunetelling
pyre—a funeral fire for burning bodies
resignation—surrender; acceptance
spoils—loot from captured places; stolen goods
valiant—brave; heroic

ACHILLES
AND HECTOR

from *THE ILIAD*

**Some history books
make war seem the story
of only weapons, battle plans,
and dates. But the Greeks
knew that war is also
the story of individuals
such as Achilles and Hector.
The day fate brings these
two great warriors together,
a ten-year-old war
is decided.**

Patroclus approached Achilles' hut with tears in his eyes.[1] As he watched his dear friend, Achilles' own heart ached. He knew why Patroclus was crying. And he knew there was nothing he could do.

[1] (pa trō′ klus) (a kil′ lēz)

"Patroclus," said Achilles, "come inside. Tell me what troubles you." Patroclus wearily stepped inside.

"You know what troubles me," said Patroclus.

Achilles nodded.

"I have heard the names of the Greeks killed in battle yesterday," said Patroclus bitterly. "Do you want to hear them too? You will recognize many of them. They were your friends—once."

Achilles lowered his head. He didn't know what to say. It was still morning. There would be more fighting and more dying in the hours ahead.

"The Trojans[2] fight well," continued Patroclus. "And the gods themselves have turned against us. Soon the Trojans will reach the shore. They will burn the Greek ships—including yours. Not one of us will see home again."

"I will fight when they reach my ships," said Achilles firmly. "You know what I have sworn. My men and I will join the battle only when we, ourselves, are threatened. Until then, I will not lift a finger to help the Greeks."

"But they cannot win without you!" Patroclus protested. "You are their champion, their only hope."

"They should have thought of that before they stirred my anger. Come, Patroclus. Whose side are you on? Theirs or mine?"

Patroclus sat in long silence before he spoke. "I must take their side this once," he said. "If you won't come yourself, allow me to fight. And allow me to lead your men into battle. Like me, they are heartbroken at the deaths of their **comrades**."

Achilles sighed. "Is this really what you want? And is this what my men want, too?"

Patroclus nodded.

"Then go," said Achilles simply. "And lead them with all the courage I know you possess."

Patroclus hesitated. "I have something else to ask. It may be a hard favor for you to grant."

---

[2](trō′ janz)

"Tell me," said Achilles.

"I am no match for you as a warrior. No man alive is—except, perhaps, for Hector.[3] We have only one hope. The Trojans must believe that you are leading them."

"And how will you make them believe that?"

Patroclus paused again. The words didn't come easily. "I want to wear your armor into battle," he said at last. "If the Trojans think that I am you, we stand a chance."

Achilles was startled by his friend's request. For someone else to wear his armor into battle. . .

But how could he refuse? How could he **deprive** his comrades of their only hope for victory?

"Go, my friend," he said, "and wear my armor. But be careful. Lead my men bravely, but don't go too far. Drive the Trojans away from the ships. After that, return to me. Do not pursue them."

Then, trying to make a joke, Achilles added, "Don't try to be a hero."

But Patroclus didn't laugh. So Achilles clasped his friend's hand and said, "Your life is very precious to me."

Quickly and quietly then, Patroclus **donned** Achilles' armor. It was grand and beautiful, yet frightening. The suit never failed to terrify the Trojans.

Before he left for battle, Patroclus halted at the entrance. "Achilles . . . the Greeks are saying you refuse to fight because you are afraid," he said.

"Afraid of what?" asked Achilles.

"A **prophecy**."

"And what prophecy is that?"

"Your own mother spoke it," said Patroclus. "She said you are fated to kill Hector in battle. Not long after that, you yourself will die."

Achilles merely grunted.

"Can it be possible this is why you do not fight?" Patroclus asked softly. "Because you are afraid of death?"

Achilles felt his anger rise. "You know very well why I

[3](hek′ tor)

don't fight," he said. "And it has nothing to do with Hector. I will kill him and die myself when my time comes. I fear no prophecy."

"Of course, my friend," said Patroclus warmly. "I'm sorry I said it. Now I must go."

After Patroclus left for battle, Achilles sat alone in his hut. Strange thoughts chased through his mind.

"Can it be?" he wondered. "Can it be that I really am afraid of Hector? But no. I know I'll kill him someday; I'm the better warrior. Yet perhaps I fear what the prophecy says will come after . . . "

But Achilles knew this wasn't so. "After all," he muttered, "what man isn't going to die? No. I fear nothing in the world. Not even death. Only Agamemnon's[4] greed pens me in this hut."

Achilles thought about that wound to his pride. Not long ago, the Greeks had seemed certain of victory. But then Agamemnon, the leader of the Greek forces, did a shameful thing. His soldiers had raided the Trojan temple of Apollo.[5] They brought the priest's daughter to Agamemnon, and Agamemnon kept her captive.

The priest begged again and again for Agamemnon to return his daughter. But foolishly, Agamemnon wouldn't listen.

So Apollo himself struck back by bringing terrible disease upon the Greeks. Many died as a result. All hope of winning the war seemed lost.

Finally Achilles had stepped forward. He demanded that Agamemnon return the girl to her father.

Agamemnon **grudgingly** agreed. But to make up for his own loss, he demanded something in return. So he took a Trojan girl who had been given to Achilles as his share of the **spoils**.

Achilles was stunned by this insult and injustice. Agamemnon had no right to take the share Achilles had

[4](ag a mem' non)
[5](a pol' lō) Apollo was the god of light and music. He was also the source of prophecy and never spoke untruthfully.

earned. That was a dishonor that no warrior could tolerate!

Since that day, proud Achilles had refused to fight with the Greeks. Yet now, watching his best friend stride off to fight, he wondered, "Did I do the right thing?"

He turned it over in his mind. "Don't I deserve a shred of dignity? Must I fight side by side with a man who has shamed me?

"No," he concluded. "I made the right choice. And I will stand by it. Not until fate forces me will I return to the battle."

He stared at the sky through the door. "In this world, there are too few choices to be made. The gods make almost all our decisions for us. So my fate is already set. The gods will choose the time and the place for me to fight again. But by what trick will they **lure** me into battle?"

In the distance, Achilles could hear the sounds of war. The rattle of spears and swords floated over the breeze. Achilles believed he could even hear Patroclus yelling orders.

Achilles prayed quietly to Zeus,[6] the king of the gods. "Zeus, you have always listened to my prayers," he whispered. "You have helped me in the past. Please watch over my friend now and send him back safely."

As he watched the battle from the heavens, Zeus heard Achilles' prayer. But it wasn't fated that he should answer. For another god took command of the battle that day. That god was Apollo, protector of the Trojans.

While Achilles prayed, Patroclus led his men against the Trojans. When they saw Achilles' gleaming armor, the Trojans were filled with fear. They believed the Greeks' greatest champion had returned to the field. They fled across the plain in blind panic.

In the excitement of victory, Patroclus forgot Achilles' orders. Though the Greek ships were safe again, Patroclus didn't stop there. He led Achilles' men after the enemy toward the walls of Troy.[7]

The god Apollo was waiting on those walls, invisible to

[6](zūs)
[7](troi)

all human eyes. He knew that the Greeks would win and destroy Troy some day. All the gods knew that. But he was determined to defend Hector and his Trojan comrades for as long as he could.

The sight of Patroclus rushing across the plain angered Apollo. "Who is this human **masquerading** as Achilles? Ah, so it's Patroclus? What makes him think he can take Troy before the gods allow it? He must be taught a lesson."

Patroclus arrived in front of Troy. He bravely tried to charge the city walls three times. But each time, Apollo threw him back. Patroclus had no idea a god was stopping him. Then, when he tried to go forward a fourth time, Apollo shouted at him.

"Stubborn fool!" said Apollo. "What do you think you're doing? Do you have it in your head to kill Hector? Would you steal that victory away from your friend Achilles? Do you think you can conquer Troy itself?

"Let me tell you this," the god continued. "Even Achilles will never break through these walls. And he's a far greater soldier than you are. So go back to your men. Leave victory over Hector and Troy to your betters."

Patroclus shook with fear. He knew he had heard the voice of a god.

"I've gone too far!" he said to himself. "Thank the gods I was warned before it was too late!"

Patroclus retreated from the wall and rejoined his comrades. He fought bravely with them and killed many Trojans. But Apollo, still angered, followed Patroclus invisibly into battle. When he saw a good moment, he knocked Patroclus down.

At first, Patroclus thought he'd been struck by an enemy soldier. He rose to his feet angrily, sword raised. But then Apollo struck him again. This time Patroclus' helmet was knocked off. It rattled across the ground.

Still unseen, Apollo lifted Patroclus to his feet and shook him violently. Patroclus' spear broke in his hands. His shield fell to the ground and his armor came loose. Dizziness swept over him. Finally he slipped to the ground.

"The unfairness of it!" Patroclus moaned. "To be beaten by an immortal god! To have no chance to fight back!"

At that moment, a Trojan soldier rushed up and drove a spear into Patroclus' back. Patroclus screamed with pain. But at least he knew it was a soldier this time, and not Apollo.

"Try again, coward!" cried Patroclus. "You haven't killed me yet! I'd rather die at mortal hands than at those of a god! At least I would have a fighting chance!"

But another soldier came to deliver Patroclus' death blow. This was Hector himself. He came running the minute he saw a man wearing Achilles' armor. Before Patroclus could rise one last time, Hector ran him through with his sword.

"At last!" cried Hector, **exulting** in the kill. "I have met the great Achilles and slain him!"

"Look again, Hector," gasped Patroclus, gazing up at Hector. "Achilles still awaits you."

"Patroclus!" exclaimed Hector. "Did Achilles put you up to this because he was afraid? So he convinced you that you could take Troy single-handedly? You thought you could kill us all? You thought you would raid our city and carry away our women? Poor fool! Your friend betrayed you into my hands!"

"Boast of my death if you like," whispered Patroclus with his dying breath. "But it was Apollo who killed me, not you. In fair combat, I could have slain you and twenty more like you. However, the gods have plans of their own. When Achilles hears of my death, you won't have long to wait. Prepare to die at his hands!"

With a final gasp, Patroclus died at Hector's feet.

Hector gazed at his enemy for a moment. Then he said quietly, "What kind of man allows himself to live in fear of prophecy? Let Achilles come. Perhaps I may yet kill him."

Then Hector stooped and stripped Patroclus' body of Achilles' armor. He proudly donned the armor. Then he turned to his soldiers.

"When Achilles comes," he said, "I'll fight him wearing his own armor! We'll see how he likes that! Now take this body of his friend and feed it to the dogs. Enough Trojans have died for his kind!"

Hector's soldiers began to carry away the body. But Achilles' men rushed upon them. They fought the Trojans fiercely, trying to win the body back. Brave Patroclus deserved a decent funeral at least. Without one, he would not find peace in the Underworld.

A horrid tug of war began, and it continued for hours. Finally, as evening approached, a messenger was sent to Achilles' hut. Achilles shivered with horror at the man's frightened face. Without being told, he knew what the messenger had come to say.

"Patroclus is dead," stammered the messenger. "Your soldiers are now fighting to get his body back—but his body only. His—your—armor has been taken."

Stunned with sadness, Achilles dropped to his knees. "But how?" he exclaimed. "Who did this?"

"Patroclus died bravely at the hands of Hector," said the messenger.

"Hector!" shouted Achilles. "How could Patroclus have met Hector in combat? I commanded him to only drive the Trojans away from the ships! Then he was supposed to return."

"He was too **valiant** to obey such orders," said the messenger. "He led your men to the very walls of Troy. If some god hadn't interfered, he might have taken the city."

Achilles wailed with despair. He gathered up the earth in his hands and poured it over his head.

The alarmed messenger quickly grabbed Achilles and held him fast. He feared Achilles might kill himself.

"Let go of me, you fool!" cried Achilles. "Do you think I'd take my own life now? No, by the gods! I refuse to die until my friend is **avenged**! Let me join the battle for Patroclus' body!"

"Leave that fight to your men," said the messenger. "You must live long enough to kill Hector."

Achilles lay on the ground, helpless with grief. "So this is the gods' grand trick!" he moaned. "This is how they will get me to fight—and die! And now, I must kill Hector because the gods say so. And then I must be killed for the same reason! What kind of heroism is this, to have no choices in the world?"

Achilles' mother, the sea goddess Thetis,[8] heard his weeping. She rushed across the seas to comfort him.

"Why are you crying, my son?" she said, gently stroking his brow. "The Greeks are in desperate need of you. And great Agamemnon himself will come to make peace with you soon. Isn't this what you wanted all along?"

"It's what I thought I wanted," cried Achilles. "But I didn't think the price would be the life of my closest friend."

"Dear son," said Thetis, "rejoin the battle if you must. But don't fight against Hector. You know you're doomed to die not long after you kill him. Perhaps you can lead the Greeks to victory without his death."

"Don't waste words, Mother," said Achilles. "I have a friend to avenge. I'd rather die than let Hector live."

"Then I won't try to stop you," said Thetis sadly. "Only do one favor for me. Don't go to fight him until dawn. In the meantime, I will go to the god Hephaestus.[9] He will make new armor for you."

Achilles agreed, and Thetis vanished into the growing dark. Achilles could hear the battle raging in the distance.

"Can I stand by while Patroclus' body is torn limb from limb?" he asked himself. "Yet I promised my mother not to fight before dawn. Still, perhaps I can be of some help, even if I don't join in the battle."

So Achilles climbed to the top of a hilltop to view the fight. The sight of bloody **carnage** greeted his eyes. Bodies of wounded and dying men were scattered everywhere. And

[8](thē' tis)
[9](he fes' tus) Hephaestus was the god of the forge and metalworking.

there in the distance, Achilles saw the struggle over Patroclus' body.

Outraged, Achilles called out, "Trojans! If you call yourselves men, surrender my friend's body!"

His voice sent chills through everyone who heard it. Even Achilles was surprised. Little did he realize that the goddess Athena[10] had come to his aid. She surrounded him with glowing light and made his voice ring like a trumpet.

The frightened Trojans let Patroclus' body fall. At once the Greeks picked it up and carried it from the field.

As his men left the field, Achilles called out to the Trojans again. "Tell Hector we will meet tomorrow! And tell him I'll make certain of his death!"

With those words, the battle ended for the day. And a sad night began. Both Greeks and Trojans had lost many noble men.

That night, Polydamas[11] paid Hector a visit. He was the prince's wisest companion.

"Hector, my friend," said Polydamas, "I was on the field today when Achilles appeared. He has forgotten his anger toward Agamemnon. He is angry only at you. And now that he is back on the field, we are in great danger. He could single-handedly defeat us."

"What is your point?" asked Hector.

"I believe it would be wise for us to leave these plains," said Polydamas. "We should go back to the city. We will be safer within its walls."

Hector angrily shook his head. "This is cowardly talk, Polydamas! Tomorrow we'll fight and drive the Greeks to their ships again! And Achilles and I will meet at last. The world will learn which of us is the better soldier. But I'll hear no more talk of hiding within the city walls!"

Many Trojans stood by, listening to Hector's words. They applauded Hector, not Polydamas. Foolishly, they failed to grasp the danger Polydamas spoke of.

---

[10] (a thē' na) Athena was a goddess of war as well as of wisdom and knowledge.
[11] (po lid' a mas)

And for good reason. Athena had stepped in again, clouding the judgment of Hector and his men. She was setting the stage for Hector's ruin. Tomorrow was to be an evil day for Troy.

Early the next morning, Thetis returned to her son as she had promised. She brought the handsome suit of armor Hephaestus had made. Sadly she watched as Achilles donned it.

"It's such beautiful armor, Mother," said Achilles. "Worthy of the greatest hero. Why should the sight of it make you sad?"

"Hephaestus said it would make you **invulnerable**," Thetis said. "I wish that were true. All your life, I've tried to keep you safe from harm. When you were a baby, I dipped you in the River Styx.[12] That should have made you an immortal like myself."

"Then perhaps you succeeded!" said Achilles, laughing. "Well, if the water of the Styx doesn't protect me, this armor surely will."

"No, child," said Thetis, near tears. "I have failed you somehow. The prophecy says so. I don't know how. And when I learn, it will be too late to correct my mistake. You will be dead."

She embraced her son, knowing it was for the last time. "Act wisely, Achilles," she said. "Before you fight, be sure to make peace with Agamemnon."

Then Thetis vanished into the sea. At once Achilles did as she suggested by calling all the Greeks together. As Agamemnon approached, Achilles felt small and foolish. Why had he stayed angry for so long? Why had he allowed so much destruction to take place? And why had he allowed his dearest friend to die?

The soldiers watched joyfully as Achilles and Agamemnon clasped hands.

"My comrade Agamemnon," said Achilles, "it seems I am always acting out of rage. Any good I do comes out of

[12](stiks) The Styx is one of the rivers of the Underworld.

rage. And so does any evil. But my rage toward you was foolish and misplaced. I beg your pardon.''

"I, too, behaved stupidly," said Agamemnon. "And soon I will shower you with treasures to make up for it. As for now, let's all eat and drink heartily! Fighting never goes well on an empty stomach.''

"You and the men can eat your fill," said Achilles. "You have my blessings. But as for myself, I have sworn not to eat or drink until Patroclus is avenged.''

And so the Greeks ate while Achilles sat alone, waiting and grieving.

A short while later, the Greeks stormed across the plains. The Trojans fought bravely. But Achilles was like an army unto himself. The other Greeks were cheered and fought better than they ever had. They were glad their champion had returned to the field.

Hector watched in **anguish** as Achilles slew one after another of his countrymen. There was no hint of mercy in Achilles' eyes. Hector could see nothing but rage there. And Hector knew who was the object of that rage.

"What can I do?" he wondered. "I can see now that Polydamas was right. We should have fled to the city walls. But it's too late for that. And how could I admit my mistake to everyone?''

Hector's mind raced, trying to think of what to do. "Perhaps I should go to Achilles, unarmed and defenseless. Yes, perhaps I should surrender. After all, the battle is clearly lost.''

But then he glimpsed again the anger in Achilles' eyes. "I am a fool," muttered Hector. "This man is mad with rage. The word 'surrender' means nothing to him. His only wish is to kill every last one of us. So I must fight him— and hope for the best.''

At that very moment, Achilles caught sight of Hector. Achilles rushed toward the prince of Troy.

So terrifying was Achilles in his armor that Hector was shaken with fear. This was death coming for him!

Suddenly mighty Hector broke into a run. Around the long walls of Troy he ran. And right behind came Achilles. Three times they circled the city.

From the heavens, Zeus watched the scene. He pitied great Hector, who had always honored the gods. "Must this hero die?" he asked the other gods. "Come, let me hear your advice."

At once Athena scolded her father. "That has already been decided," she said. "It is Hector's day to die. Achilles' day will also come before long."

"Perhaps so, daughter," said Zeus. "But let me test this decision one more time." So Zeus raised his golden scales. Then he placed the deaths of Hector and Achilles on each side. Hector's was the heavier, and dropped low.

"Very well," sighed Zeus sadly. "Hector will die today."

Athena was thrilled at her father's words. She hurriedly turned to Apollo. "We'll have no more **meddling** from you today," she said with a glare. "When a human's death is fated, no god may interfere."

"This won't stop *your* meddling, I'm sure," sneered Apollo.

"I'll just make sure everything happens as it is fated!" said Athena, laughing. "I can do whatever I like, as long as it doesn't go against fate!"

Then she rushed back to the battlefield. She found Achilles still pursuing Hector around the city.

Suddenly Achilles heard the voice of the goddess speaking in his ear. "You can stop this endless chase," Athena told him. "All the gods know that this is the day of Hector's death. And I, myself, will hand him over for the kill! Just stand and wait. And make sure your spear is ready!"

Achilles, surprised by Athena's words, did as he was told. Then Athena took the form of Hector's beloved brother Deiphobus.[13] She appeared right in Hector's path.

When Hector saw her in this form, he stopped dead in his tracks. "Brother!" he cried, panting for breath. "Why

---

[13] (dē if' o bus or de if' o bus)

aren't you safely in the city with our mother and father?''

"I've come to fight with you," said Athena in Deiphobus' voice. "I know you wish to fight Achilles by yourself. But I couldn't leave you alone. Perhaps Achilles is too strong for the both of us. So be it. I would rather die at your side."

Tears came to Hector's eyes. "Dear brother, how can I say no? To fight together will be an honor, whether in victory or defeat!"

And so Hector turned to face Achilles, who was waiting close by. "Achilles, I am too tired to flee anymore. Now we must fight, and one of us must die. But let's make a bargain first. If you die at my hands, I'll return your body to your men—after I've taken your splendid armor. I only ask that you do the same for me. Please grant this last request. Before we die, let's try to behave like men."

"Men!" snarled Achilles. "There are no men left on this field! We're all animals stalking one another, thirsting for each other's blood. There's no use in talking about bargains.

"The gods themselves have destroyed all bargains, and all friendship. They watch us die for their amusement. The goddess Athena is near, and she will hand you over to me. Just remember this. When you killed Patroclus, you killed all mercy inside me."

With these words, Achilles raised his spear and hurled it. Hector dodged it skillfully. But Hector didn't see Athena pick up the spear and return it to Achilles.

"You have missed, great Achilles!" Hector exclaimed. "It seems you didn't know my fate as well as you thought! Now dodge my spear if you can. I pray that it may hit you. Then my Trojans might have a fighting chance to win this war!"

So saying, Hector hurled his own spear at Achilles. But it bounced off Achilles' shield and fell too far away for Hector to reach.

Hector was angry that his shot had not struck. He turned and called for his brother.

"Deiphobus!" he cried. "I need your spear!"

But, of course, his brother was not there. Nothing was there except the bloody battlefield.

Hector knew then that his brother had been but an illusion. Achilles' words were true.

"So, the gods have decided my hour of death is come," he said softly. "I cannot avoid my fate. Yet at least I can die bravely."

Hector drew his sword and charged at Achilles one last time. Achilles watched him carefully as he approached. He was the only man alive who knew the weak place in Hector's armor. After all, that armor had once been Achilles'.

The unprotected spot was at Hector's throat. So when Hector came near enough, Achilles drove his spear there. It was a death blow, and Hector fell to the ground with a gasp.

"So, Hector," **gloated** Achilles. "I've paid you in full for the death of Patroclus. My friend will be properly buried. But you'll be left for the dogs and birds!"

"I beg you, don't leave me for the dogs," Hector pleaded. "Let my mother and father have my body. They'll give you fine gifts in return."

"You dog!" Achilles spit back. "I wish I could eat your flesh myself! Never will I ransom your body. Not even if your father promised your weight in gold. No, your mother will never place your body on a proper bed to grieve for you!"

The darkness of death closed around Hector. As life left him, he said, "I can see I wasn't fated to persuade you. Your heart is iron, Achilles. But now it is you who must prepare for death. The day will come when my brother Paris[14] and mighty Apollo will kill you. Nor will all your courage put off that day."

Hector's eyes clouded over and his breathing stopped. Achilles stared at his dead foe. Though he knew Hector's words were true, he was beyond fear. Rage seemed to be the only thing he could feel.

"Let death come when it may," he whispered to Hector's

---

[14] (pa′ ris)

dead body. "Revenge is my only desire. And I'm not through revenging myself on you."

Then he stripped off the armor that Hector wore. As he did so, the Greeks crowded round. In silent wonder, they stared at the godlike body of their foe.

Suddenly one man darted forward. With a savage thrust, he sank his spear into Hector's body. Quickly others followed, wounding the body again and again. As they stabbed at the once great hero, they laughed. "This Hector is easier to handle now than when he was at our ships with those torches."

After collecting the armor, Achilles pierced Hector's feet and bound them together. Then, tying the body to his chariot, Achilles drove off as fast as he could. Round Troy he rode, dragging Hector's body behind.

Above on the walls, Hector's family and people watched and wept. Loyal son, gentle husband, loving father, kind brother, brave defender. The greatest Trojan of all was dead. And now to be treated so shamefully by Achilles! The echoes of their cries drifted like ghosts over the plain.

At last Achilles left the field and returned to camp. There he threw Hector's body in front of Patroclus' body. And he summoned all the Greeks to a grand funeral feast in his friend's honor.

Yet Achilles' victory seemed empty. After the others went to sleep, Achilles tossed and turned. Finally he went down to the beach and angrily wept.

"I thought revenge would make me forget my grief," he moaned. "I thought I could erase the memory of the way I failed Patroclus. But these tears will not stop!"

At last Achilles lay down in the sand, weary from fighting and weeping. He slept long and deeply. But he was awakened by a voice.

"Achilles, arise," it said. "Help me. Please."

Achilles looked up in amazement. Patroclus was standing in front of him.

"Have I awakened from some nightmare?" exclaimed

Achilles. "Was your death just some terrible dream?"

"I am as dead as when you last saw me," said Patroclus sadly. "I am Patroclus' shade and nothing more. And you, my friend, have failed me bitterly."

"I know!" cried Achilles. "Oh, how well I know! I should never have let you go into battle!"

"That isn't what I meant," replied Patroclus. "My body still lies unburied."

"Oh, I'm sorry for that, my friend! But my first concern was to avenge your death. And I have done so! Hector is dead! Surely you can rest easier because of that."

Patroclus smiled a bitter smile. "Poor Achilles," he said. "Revenge is much more important to the living than the dead. All we want is peace. Soon, my friend, you'll understand. But for now, please put my body to rest."

"I will do that," promised Achilles. "And I'll instruct my men to bury my body with yours. Farewell, my friend."

With those words, Achilles reached out to embrace Patroclus. But the shade vanished into thin air. Achilles fell to his knees in tears. As the night passed on, he slept and wept, slept and wept.

When morning came, Achilles gathered his men together. They built a funeral **pyre** upon which they burned Patroclus' body.

To that fire, they added the bodies of sheep, horses, cattle, and dogs. Then Achilles himself cut the throats of twelve Trojan captives. All these bodies were placed on the funeral pyre.

When the mighty blaze had died down, they placed the ashes in a tomb. After that, the Greeks played athletic games and contests in Patroclus' honor.

Yet Achilles' grief and anger still would not fade. For days after, he dragged Hector's body behind his chariot. He charged wildly about the plain. Over and over he screamed his rage to the heavens themselves.

The gods heard Achilles' ravings and watched the scene from above. Many of them were displeased. They disliked to see the dead mistreated so. At last Apollo spoke to Zeus, expressing his unhappiness.

"The prophecy has unfolded as it was supposed to," Apollo said. "And I have been careful not to interfere. But how can any of us stand by and watch this? We have granted Achilles victory. Now he behaves like a **barbarian.** So far, I have managed to keep Hector's body from harm. But how long must this continue?"

"Your words are wise," Zeus agreed. "Achilles has carried his anger too far. But I know how to bring him to his senses. A father's grief is all that's needed."

Zeus called Hermes,[15] the messenger god, to his side. "Go to old Priam,[16] the king of Troy and Hector's father. Lead him to Achilles' hut. See that he comes to no harm."

In an instant, Hermes had flown to Troy. He found Priam already on his way to the Grecian camp. The king was driving a wagon full of rich clothing, goblets, rugs, and gold. All of Troy's greatest treasures were in that wagon. And every last item Priam intended to offer Achilles for the return of Hector's body.

Priam pulled to a stop when he saw Hermes. The messenger god, who had taken the form of a handsome youth, approached.

"Ho, old father. Where are you headed? Surely not to the Greek camp?"

"Yes, my son. I hope to move Achilles' heart with my tears—and this treasure."

Hermes shook his head. "As Achilles' servant, I warn you that your mission won't be easy."

"You have come from Achilles?" asked Priam. "Then you must take me back with you to his hut. I cannot bear watching my son suffer, even in death."

"But do you dare face Achilles?" asked Hermes.

"I am an old man," sighed Priam. "My own death is due before long. What have I to fear?"

---

[15] (her' mēz)
[16] (prī' am)

So the wing-footed Hermes showed Priam to Achilles' hut. There the god finally revealed himself.

"Now I must leave you, King Priam," Hermes said at the end of his explanation. "A god should not be seen begging favors of a mortal."

Priam nodded. "It will not be necessary, in any case. A grieving father needs no god to tell him what to say."

Old Priam entered the hut and knelt down before Achilles. Then to the surprise of all, Priam kissed Achilles' hands. He kissed those hands that had murdered so many of his sons.[17]

"Greetings, Achilles," said Priam, his voice shaking with grief. "I have come to reclaim my son."

Achilles rose to his feet. The sight of this sad old man filled him with strange emotions. He could say nothing.

"Remember," said Priam, "that you have a father, too—an old man like myself. He will grieve as I do when you die. And that time, they say, is very near. Would you wish him to see your body dragged and **mutilated** so?"

Still silent, Achilles felt his eyes fill with tears. His throat burned with sadness.

"This man you've killed," Priam continued, "had a mother to mourn him. A wife, too—a beloved wife."

Priam's voice suddenly broke. "And a son. Did you know that? Yes, a little son. I remember one day that Hector left for battle. He came to say goodbye to his boy. But the child was frightened by Hector's gleaming helmet. He drew back and cried. And Hector laughed. He took off his helmet and picked up his babe, kissing him sweetly. . . . My dear son, he only laughed."

The two men stood quietly for a moment.

"Children know so much more than we do, don't they?" said Achilles.

Priam nodded silently. A sad smile crossed his face.

"I have been a soldier all my life," said Achilles, his voiced choked with emotion. "But I have never witnessed bravery like yours. When I look upon your tears, I see my

[17] Priam had fifty sons.

own tears for Patroclus. I also see, for the first time, that all tears are alike. And for the first time, I feel free. Free of anger, free of rage.

"The gods have directed my every action—except my grieving. And now you and I can grieve together while the gods do nothing but watch. They cannot stop us. Yes, old man. To share our grief is the only freedom we have left."

Achilles and Priam embraced each other, weeping. Then in honorable fashion, Priam presented Achilles with his treasure. In return, Achilles tenderly gave back the body of Priam's son.

The two armies agreed to stop fighting for a time. It took the Trojans ten days to build a funeral pyre worthy of Hector. And on the eleventh day, his body was burned. In peace at last, his soul was allowed to enter the Underworld.

Then, on the twelfth day, the fighting began again.

Not long after that, Achilles led his army in a mighty charge. Like his friend Patroclus, he reached the gates of Troy.

Hector's brother, Paris, awaited Achilles on the walls of Troy. When Achilles came in sight, Paris fired a fateful arrow. For Apollo was standing by Paris' side, ready to avenge Hector's death. The god directed the arrow's path to Achilles heel.

The arrow dove deep. And Achilles fell to the ground, knowing that death was upon him.

"Dear mother," he whispered as his life fled away. "Now the prophecy comes true, though you tried to prevent it. When you placed me in the River Styx, you held me by my heel. And in that place only could I be killed. But do not grieve, for it isn't your fault. Fate decides all. Farewell."

Achilles' whispering faded into silence. His world went black. In shock and horror the Greeks and Trojans watched him die. Then within moments, they were fighting again, struggling to win his body.

But Achilles was free of rage at last. All that was left was **resignation**.

INSIGHTS

Achilles is probably the greatest warrior of Greek myth. And with a few different genes, he might have ruled Olympus as well.

The story of Achilles' birth is linked with the Titan Prometheus. For many years, Prometheus and Zeus carried on a long feud. Zeus even ended up chaining Prometheus to a mountain. Finally their argument ended when Zeus allowed Prometheus to be freed.

In turn, Prometheus revealed a great secret. He warned Zeus not to take the nymph Thetis as a lover. He knew that Thetis would bear a son greater than the father of her child.

Upon hearing this, Zeus hastily stopped pursuing Thetis. The god gladly blessed Thetis' marriage to Peleus, who became Achilles' father.

Thetis had the privilege of knowing the future. But it proved a bitter gift, since she foresaw her son's death at Troy.

To prevent this, she disguised her son as a girl at King Lycomedes' court. In this way she hoped to hide Achilles from Greek recruiters.

But Odysseus (who was also dragged into the Trojan War) unmasked Achilles. He suspected what Thetis had done and went to visit Lycomedes. With him, Odysseus brought gifts for the king's daughters. Among the gifts were a shield and spear.

The clever Odysseus then raised a battle cry. Thinking they were under attack, Achilles seized the weapons. With that one gesture, Achilles revealed himself. And without further protest, he went to meet his fate at Troy.

As the myth relates, Achilles' one weak spot was his heel. The *Achilles' tendon,* located at the back of the ankle, gets its name from the Greek warrior. A person whose ankle tendon is cut has trouble walking and is not able to stand on tiptoe. Today, any weak point is known as an *Achilles' heel.*

If Achilles is remembered for his weakness, Hector has suffered an even worse fate. In Greek myth, Hector was portrayed as noble and brave. He killed at least thirty-one of the best Greek warriors before being slain by Achilles. But strangely enough, *hector* now means "to act like a bully."

Before 1868, most historians doubted that Troy ever existed. But in that year, German businessman Heinrich Schliemann found traces of an ancient city where Troy was thought to be located. Bronze armor and swords, as described in the myths, were found at the site. And it appeared that the city was once destroyed by fire—just like the Troy of myths. Many scholars now agree that Troy really existed and was destroyed in a war around 1250-1150 B.C.

THE TROJAN HORSE

VOCABULARY PREVIEW

Below is a list of words that appear in the story. Read the list and get to know the words before you start the story.

apparition—ghost
assailants—opponents; attackers
confounded—confused; puzzled
devious—sly; tricky
doused—soaked
futile—useless; unsuccessful
inferno—hell-like place; extreme heat
livid—very angry; furious
lodged—stuck
lulled—quieted; calmed
plight—bad condition; difficult situation
ravaged—destroyed; ruined
reign—to rule
revel—wild time; drinking spree
rubble—broken pieces of stone from a crumbling building
sanctuary—safety; shelter
sarcastically—mockingly
shrine—temple; sacred place
taunted—made fun of; mocked
wily—sly; clever

THE TROJAN -HORSE-

from *THE AENEID*

Not every battle is won by brute force. Sometimes a deadly trick works better than the biggest weapon. And who will be left to say it's unfair if the trick succeeds?

I t was dawn. The Trojans[1] stared in stunned silence at the plain in front of their city. To the west of their gates stood a gigantic wooden horse. This statue towered even higher than the walls of their city. No Trojan had ever seen anything like it. What was it?

[1] (trō′ janz)

But something else **confounded** them even more. Beyond the horse, they could see the plains leading to the sea. Those plains were empty. And so were the waters beyond.

Just yesterday, the Greek army had been camped by the sea. Their huts had filled the countryside, and their ships had crowded the beach. For ten long years the Trojans had faced that sight.

Now the people broke into cheers of joy.

"The Greeks are gone!" cried one.

"We've won the war at last!" shouted another.

"Who cares who won or lost?" yelled still another. "We have peace again! Peace after ten years of endless bloodshed!"

The Trojans threw open their gates and rushed out onto the plain. They ran to the Greeks' campsite and happily pointed at the various huts.

"And where are they now, those brave warriors?" they laughed. "Run away like rabbits, every one of them!"

But then the great horse caught their eye again. It stood squarely before the gate, glaring at the city behind the walls.

The Trojans gathered around it in wonder. "What can it mean?" asked one.

"It must be a gift of peace, left by the Greeks," answered another. "Let's take it inside our walls. We should give it a place of honor."

This suggestion was followed by a burst of bitter laughter. The Trojans turned and looked to the city walls. There stood the great priest Laocoon,[2] a grim smile on his face.

"A gift of peace from the Greeks!" he cried **sarcastically**. "Oh, yes, that makes sense! For ten long years they bleed us. One by one they kill our heroes. They fight until almost every god in the heavens joins their cause. And then they vanish into the night, leaving us a gift! But of course! How logical!"

Laocoon stamped his foot. "What nonsense!" he cried. "Do as I say or you'll surely die. Take their gift, set it afire,

[2](lā ok′ ō on)

and throw it into the sea. I tell you it is an evil thing. I don't trust the Greeks—even when they bear gifts!''

And with those words, Laocoon hurled his spear. It struck the horse and **lodged** in its side. The horse echoed with a weird, hollow sound.

The Trojans moved nearer the horse, examining it more closely. Old Priam, the king of Troy, joined the crowd and stood among them.[3] For all his wisdom, he was as confounded as the rest.

Then the silence was broken by shouting. The crowd parted to let three men into their midst. Two of them were Trojan shepherds. The third was a Greek soldier, his hands tied behind his back.

When they reached the gate, the shepherds threw the soldier to the ground. He gazed at the Trojans in terror, tears of fear in his eyes.

The Trojan boys quickly surrounded the soldier. With laughter and insults, they **taunted** the prisoner.

"Please, don't hurt me," begged the soldier. "The Greeks have betrayed me. They've left me here to die!''

Priam raised his hand, and the crowd's shouts died to murmurs. "Speak, man," he said. "Tell us who you are and why you're still here."

"My name is Sinon,"[4] moaned the soldier. "But why do you ask to hear my story? You don't care about me. All you want to do is to kill me. Well, do it then! Believe me, nothing could make the Greeks happier than my death!''

A hush fell over the crowd. Suddenly everyone wanted to know Sinon's story.

"Tell us," said Priam gently. "Perhaps your words will save your life."

"Very well then," said Sinon. "You know how the goddess Athena[5] once supported the Greeks in this war. And you also know how our general Odysseus[6] stole her statue

[3] (prī' am) (troi)
[4] (sī' non)
[5] (a thē' na) Athena was the goddess of war and of wisdom and knowledge.
[6] (ō dis' ūs or ō dis' sē us)

from your temple. Great fool! The goddess turned against us then.

"Well, after that, the Greeks despaired of ever winning. All they wanted to do was go home. But the weather was never fit for sailing. Terrible storms came, followed by windless days. So the Greeks asked their prophet, Calchas,[7] what to do.

"Old Calchas told them unsettling news. He said they must sacrifice one of their own warriors to the gods. Only then would the winds turn to their favor. You can well imagine the Greeks were unhappy to hear this!

"Each man wondered who should be sacrificed. At long last, Odysseus demanded that Calchas choose the man. Calchas remained silent for days and days. But at last he named the man. And it was me!

"If you ask me, the whole thing was a plot," Sinon said, his voice now angry. "Odysseus always hated me. And I think he paid off Calchas to do me in. But who'd believe me? The other men didn't care in the least. They were happy enough not to be chosen themselves. My death didn't matter to them.

"It mattered to me, though. So when the day came for my sacrifice, I made a run for it. The Greeks looked high and low, but never found me. That's because I outsmarted them—even cunning Odysseus. I hid myself underwater in the swamps until they passed.

"At last the Greeks gave up their search. Bad winds or no, they decided to sail on."

Sinon turned his pleading eyes on the crowd. "Kill me then. But know that the Greeks will be most pleased to see my blood. And if Calchas spoke true, you'll help them on their way."

Priam almost wept at poor Sinon's **plight**. Indeed, some of the Trojans did shed tears.

"Listen to me, young man," said Priam. "The Greeks may have betrayed you, but we shall not. Consider yourself

[7](kal′ kas)

a citizen of Troy. From now on, you are one of us.''

Then he commanded the shepherds to untie Sinon. They obeyed.

''But you haven't told us everything, Sinon,'' said Priam. ''What is this horse, and where did it come from?''

Sinon was quiet for a moment. He seemed afraid to speak. Finally he said, ''I hope you spoke truthfully about giving me **sanctuary**. I'm lost if I'm not a citizen of Troy. For I'm about to tell you the greatest secret of the Greeks.''

The Trojans listened breathlessly as Sinon continued.

''When the Greeks learned of Athena's anger, they turned to Calchas for advice. He commanded them to build this horse as a gift to her. 'Be sure to make it big,' Calchas said. 'Make it so huge that the Trojans can't get it into their city. If they ever do, they'll receive Athena's favor for themselves.'

''The Greeks did as Calchas commanded. But as things turned out, the gift wasn't enough. Calchas told them they must sail back to Greece. There they are to wait for a sign from the gods. And when that sign comes, the Greeks will be back. They'll fight again—and win.

''That's the truth, I swear it,'' concluded Sinon. ''The Greeks are hoping for two things. First, they hope that you'll kill me. Second, they pray you'll destroy this horse. So if you do either, your city is doomed.''

Sinon gazed at the horse. ''Still, what a shame you can't take the beast within your walls!'' he added with a sigh. ''Calchas says you'd be the victors if you did. Then it would be you who could sail for Greece and destroy them!''

Sinon's words rang true to all the Trojans who heard them. Yet they were cautious. The great horse looked so threatening. Did they dare take it within the walls of Troy?

Laocoon saw it was no use talking. Angry at being ignored, he went back to his temple. With his two sons by his side, he sacrificed a bull to Athena.

Yet even as Laocoon was busy with such sacred acts, horror was brewing. As the Trojans outside the city watched, two huge serpents came out of the sea. The hideous creatures raced across the plain into the city.

The Trojans hesitated and then followed the snakes. Straight to the temple the serpents went. With lightning speed they wrapped themselves around Laocoon and his sons. Two quick bites killed the boys. Then the snakes crushed the priest to death. Their grim work done, the serpents vanished inside the temple.

The watching Trojans screamed in terror.

"This is the price Laocoon paid for speaking against the horse!" cried one.

"That ill-thrown spear cost him his life!" cried a second.

Immediately the Trojans started to tear an opening in the wall. They made a hole big enough to get the great horse through. Then they raised the wooden monster onto wheels and began pushing and pulling forward.

The horse shook and swayed as the Trojans tugged. But little by little, it rolled into the city.

With all the shouting and thunder of the wheels, no one was listening very carefully. So the suspicious noises inside the horse's belly went unheard.

That evening was one of great celebration in Troy. There was singing, feasting, and drinking. The Trojans danced, too. Round the wooden horse they circled, decorating it with flowers.

By midnight, the **revel** had exhausted everyone. Every soul in the city was fast asleep.

Every soul, that is, except for Sinon. He waited anxiously atop the walls of Troy, gazing out to sea. At last he saw a light shining in the distance.

That was his signal. Sinon scrambled down the walls and rushed to the wooden horse.

In the belly of the horse, Sinon found the carefully hidden door the Trojans had missed. He gave a quick rap on the door, then opened it.

One by one, several Greek generals leapt out of the horse. They tumbled to the ground and dusted themselves off.

The **wily** Odysseus was the first out of the horse. He was quickly followed by Neoptolemus, the son of dead Achilles.[8] Neoptolemus looked brave and fine in his father's armor.

"Odysseus, I must admit, I didn't think it would work," said Neoptolemus. "I thought we'd all be dead by now."

"I thought so myself," chuckled Odysseus. "Every time our armor rattled, I believed we were done for! But my plan has worked so far—thanks to this fine fellow here."

And with those words, Odysseus clasped Sinon by the hand.

"Well done, Sinon!" exclaimed Odysseus. "You're an excellent liar!"

Sinon blushed with pride. It was quite a compliment, coming from Odysseus. Lying was a new art in those days. Few people had mastered it. Odysseus was one of those few—and one of the finest liars ever.

"But I don't understand one thing," said Sinon. "The serpents which killed Laocoon—where did they come from?"

"Some god has taken up our side, I suppose," said Odysseus with a shrug. "But let's not stand here talking. To the gates!"

Odysseus' guess was true. Poseidon[9] had sent the serpents to help trick the Trojans. The gods often helped mortals in such **devious** ways.

The generals wasted no time. They rushed to the gates of Troy and threw them open. There they awaited the return of their army.

You see, the Greeks had not gone home at all. Instead, they had hidden their ships behind a nearby island. When nightfall came, they sailed back again. The signal Sinon had seen was a torch the army lit upon landing. Now the great army was marching silently toward the city.

They arrived at the gate without a whisper from their armor. At once they broke off in all directions to move through the city. All had the same purpose. They intended

---

[8] (nē op tol' e mus) (a kil' lēz)
[9] (pō sī' don) Poseidon was the god of the sea and the bringer of earthquakes.

to kill every man in Troy, awake or asleep.

The destruction began with fire. Sinon speedily ran about, torching every house he came to. Flames sprang up everywhere. It seemed certain that every last Trojan would die before they even knew of their danger.

But fortunately not all the Trojans had been **lulled** by their wine. The warrior Aeneas, son of Aphrodite, was sleeping fitfully.[10] Terrible nightmares kept haunting him.

At last Aeneas' eyes snapped open. But there he found a nightmare worse than those of his dreams. For at the foot of his bed stood a bloody figure. It was a Trojan soldier, battered with wounds.

After a moment, Aeneas realized he knew the figure. It was Hector,[11] prince of Troy.

"Hector, my friend!" he cried. "But this can't be! You were killed in combat with Achilles. We all saw you die. And we saw Achilles drag your body behind his chariot."

"I am dead indeed," said Hector's ghost. "But you may be saved. The Greeks are in the city and killing with a ten-year greed."

"In the city!" At once Aeneas reached for his armor and sword.

"No!" Hector shouted. "Don't try to fight. It will do no good now. The Greeks have beaten us at last—through cunning and not courage. So run. Run for your life. And take your family with you. In time, you will build a new city far away. Now flee at once."

Aeneas rubbed his eyes. When he opened them again, the **apparition** was gone. For a moment he thought he had just imagined Hector's appearance.

But then the sounds of fighting reached him. And the wind brought the choking smell of smoke.

Aeneas dashed to the windows and cried out in grief. Greek warriors were storming down the streets, killing Trojan men at every step. Everywhere houses were burning.

---

[10] (ē nē′ as) (af rō di′ tē) Aphrodite was the goddess of love and beauty.
[11] (hek′ tor)

In a flash, Aeneas understood Sinon's trick. Despite Hector's words, he ran back for his weapons.

"Brave Hector," he whispered, "you told me to run. But I cannot. I won't let the Greeks take Troy without a fight."

As he left his house, he was greeted by some of his fellow soldiers. "Our cause is lost," he told them. "But I don't wish to live to witness our defeat. And I can tell by your faces that you feel the same way. Come with me, and let's die fighting."

So a small number of Trojans fought bravely. And many Greeks died at their hands. In fact, Aeneas fought so fiercely that he and his men actually reached Priam's palace.

There they found guards standing atop the towers, loyally protecting their king. These men were using any weapon that came to hand. With stones from the roof and walls the Trojans shelled their **assailants**. And just as the Greeks were about to break down the palace doors, the Trojans struck a deadly blow. They toppled a great tower upon the attackers. Many Greeks were crushed.

But Neoptolemus managed to dodge the missile. When the dust had settled, he climbed over the **rubble** and bodies and broke through the doors. With several of his men following him, he charged toward Priam's chamber.

At that very moment, old Priam was putting on his armor. It had been many years since Priam had actually lifted a sword in battle. Now his old hands fumbled with the fastenings of his armor.

The fact that his wife, Hecuba,[12] was trying to stop him didn't help. "What do you think you're doing?" she cried. "Do you believe you can fight them all by yourself? Don't be a fool! You're too old for battle! Come to our sacred altar and pray with me. If the gods won't save us, nothing will."

"Away from me, Hecuba," replied her husband. "The Greeks must find me ready."

___

[12] (hek′ ū ba)

Knowing she couldn't change his mind, Hecuba went to the altar and prayed. And Priam took his place at the door.

In a moment, it burst open. One of Priam's sons—a mere boy—rushed into the room.

"Father, they're chasing me!" he cried. "I'd fight them, but there are too many!"

No sooner had he spoken these words than Neoptolemus stepped into the room. He grabbed the boy and ran him through with his sword. Then he threw the dead body at Priam's feet.

Priam was **livid**. His voice shook with fury. "I once met the man you call your father," he said to Neoptolemus. "Achilles was his name. He showed me mercy and respect. You don't even know the meaning of those words!

"Achilles would never have slain a mere boy before his father's eyes," Priam continued. "But you're not Achilles' son. You're a monster! You have no right to wear his armor."

Then, with what little strength he had, the old man flung his spear at Neoptolemus. It lodged in a loop of the warrior's shield.

Neoptolemus laughed. "And now, old man, you'll be going to meet my father," he sneered. "Tell him what a monster you think I am. Tell him you don't believe I'm really his son. See if he agrees with you. Then come back and tell me—if you can!"

Neoptolemus dragged King Priam to the altar where Hecuba prayed. He slew him on the spot, then left the room.

Rescue came too late. Aeneas had seen Neoptolemus enter the palace. He flew down the hallways in pursuit. But he arrived to find just the dead and the weeping. Only Queen Hecuba remained silent as she sat white-faced with shock.

Aeneas didn't need to touch the bodies of noble Priam or the boy to know they were dead. He simply stared, sickened by the sight.

"And what of my own family?" he wondered. "What of my wife, father, and child? All slain by now, surely. So there is nothing left for me except to fight and die. But first. . .''

"Hecuba—" he began.

The queen lifted her head. "They are dead," she said in a dry voice.

"My queen, you must flee this place," Aeneas urged.

She shook her head. "Where would I go? Straight into the arms of the Greeks? No, better to die here beside them."

Aeneas could see she was determined. To plead with her further would be useless. And he must get back to his family!

Aeneas rushed back into the hallway. Smoke choked his lungs. The palace was an **inferno**. He groped along, cautiously finding his way.

Acncas passed several more bodies before he found another living soul. It proved to be a woman. She was crouched weeping in a corner.

Aeneas gently lifted her head and recognized her at once. And the sight of her unearthly beauty filled him with rage.

"So Helen!" he hissed. "Weeping at last for your crimes? It was you who brought this on us! When you ran away with our prince Paris, you knew what would happen. You knew your husband wouldn't take it lightly. Indeed, he did not! No, Menelaus[13] gathered every army in Greece to come and fetch you! And so we have fought for ten long years. Now our city has been **ravaged** to the roots. And all because of you!"

Helen, too terrified to speak, gazed at him with her gorgeous eyes.

"Why are you so frightened?" sneered Aeneas. "Are you afraid of me? Or perhaps the Greeks? Oh, but they'll never kill you! You'll be their prize! You'll go home and live happily with your husband and family. You'll forget this ever happened." Aeneas spat on the floor. "By the gods, I've never killed a woman before. But if any woman deserved to die, it's you!"

Aeneas raised his sword and might have actually slain her.

[13] (men e lā′ us)

But in an instant, his goddess mother appeared before his eyes. She stayed his hand.

"Enough, Aeneas," Aphrodite said. "There's too little mercy in this city as it is. Don't rob it of any more. Helen was not the cause of this terrible war. The gods were. And now I am the only god left on Troy's side.

"All is lost for this city, my son, so do as I say. Give up this **futile** fighting. Run to your home at once and save your family. I've done everything I could to keep them alive. Now it's up to you to rescue them."

The vision vanished. Aeneas stood stunned for a moment.

"My family!" he cried. "Still alive?"

He rushed out of the palace and raced home. Inside his house, he found his old father, Anchises,[14] sitting quietly.

"Father, I've come to take you away," said Aeneas. "We still have a slim chance of escape."

"Take your wife and child," said Anchises. "But leave me here. You don't need an old man slowing you down. Don't worry over me. I'll never let the Greeks take me alive. When they come near, I'll take my own life."

Aeneas paced the room furiously. "What are you saying, Father?" he cried. "Do you expect me to run away and leave you here?"

Aeneas suddenly shouted to the skies. "Mother, listen to me! It's too late for escape, and my father refuses to come. I can't leave, knowing he'll be butchered by the Greeks. I must stay and fight."

Then Aeneas' wife, Creusa,[15] stepped before him. She held their little boy by the hand. "Fight if you will, Aeneas," she said. "But let us remain with you. Don't leave us to the Greeks."

The boy looked up at his father, trembling with fear. At that moment, a miracle took place. The child's head was lit by a soft, glowing flame.

Terrified at first, Aeneas **doused** the boy's head with

[14](an kī' sēz)
[15](krē ū' sa   or   kre ū' sa)

water. But the fire had not burned the child.

Anchises stared in wonder. "It's a sign from the gods themselves!" he cried. "Lord Zeus,[16] do you mean to save us? If you do, show us another sign to prove it!"

A sharp clap of thunder was his answer. That was followed by a shooting star that raced across the sky.

"Dear son!" exclaimed Anchises. "The gods have not forgotten us after all! I *will* come with you!"

At once Aeneas led his family out into the streets. The heat and roar of flames surrounded them.

"We have no time left," cried Aeneas. He threw a lion-skin on his back and stooped down.

"Climb on my back, Father," he said. The old man did as he was told.

"And now, boy," said Aeneas to his son, "take my hand and run beside me. Creusa, follow us. Let's go!"

They made their way through the burning streets. At last they approached the gates of Troy. But then Aeneas' father yelled out a warning.

"We can't go this way!" he cried. "I see Greek shields coming through the smoke!"

Aeneas and his family turned and ran the other way. Through the alleys and back streets they fled. They managed to avoid the Greeks and reach Demeter's[17] sacred **shrine**. They would be safe there for a time.

But then Aeneas turned and gasped with horror. His wife was gone! In his haste to rescue his son and father, he had lost her. He rushed out of the sanctuary and back into the ruined streets. Again and again he called Creusa's name.

At last, exhausted, he fell weeping to his knees. Then he heard a voice speak softly: "Don't weep, Aeneas."

Aeneas looked up. Before him stood the ghost of Creusa. He moaned with sorrow.

"I was not meant to escape with you. The gods have made other plans," Creusa said sadly. "Flee now. Take our son

---

[16](zūs) Zeus was lord of the heavens and king of the gods.
[17](de mē' ter) Demeter was the goddess of the cornfield.

and Anchises with you. You have a long journey ahead and many troubles. But great rewards await you. You will reach another land and rebuild our kingdom there. And you shall **reign** with a lovely queen."

Desperate with sorrow, Aeneas tried to embrace the apparition. But she slipped through his fingers like water.

"Do not mourn for me, Aeneas," Creusa said. "At least I have not been taken by the Greeks. I shall not have to live as a slave. Death is better."

Aeneas tried again to seize Creusa. But she vanished.

Aeneas sat weeping for a long time. Then he slowly turned back to Demeter's shrine. The burning cinders of Troy lay all around him.

To his surprise, a number of people had gathered at the shrine. These were the only Trojans who had not been captured or killed. They were anxiously awaiting his return.

"You are the only leader Troy has left," cried one. "What shall we do, Aeneas?"

Almost too weary to stand, Aeneas thought long and hard. "We will go to the mountains," he said. "We will rest and then build enough ships for us all. After that, we sail—though I don't know where. But with the help of the gods, we shall find a new home. And now, my friends, follow me."

Dawn was coming. Aeneas turned and headed for the mountains, stiff with pain and weariness. The other Trojans followed him. Together, they managed to slip past the Greeks and out of the city. Not until they reached the mountains did they stop to rest.

Eventually Aeneas would lead his loyal band to Italy. There he would found one of the greatest empires in history. Thus out of the ruins of Troy arose mighty Rome.

INSIGHTS

Though so many humans became involved, the Trojan War began with the gods. It started when at a wedding feast, trouble-making Eris (or Strife) threw down a golden apple. A tag on the apple read, "For the fairest."

Three goddesses tried to claim the prize: Hera, Athena, and Aphrodite. To settle the argument, Paris (a prince of Troy) was asked to pick the fairest.

But what Paris ended up judging was not looks but bribes. Athena, goddess of war, promised him victory against the Greeks. Hera, wife of the king of the gods, offered to make him ruler of Asia and Europe. Aphrodite, goddess of love, said the most beautiful woman in the world would be his.

Paris chose Aphrodite. His reward was the lovely Helen. Unfortunately, Helen was married to King Menelaus. So when Paris whisked her away to Troy, Menelaus gathered an army of Greeks to get her back. Thus began the Trojan War.

Neoptolemus was not the noble warrior his father, Achilles, was. Not only did Neoptolemus kill Hector's father, he also threw Hector's infant son from the walls of Troy. In addition, he captured Hector's wife and made her his slave.

Laocoon wasn't the only Trojan to suspect the horse. Cassandra also knew of the trick—as she knew all of the future. Apollo had given her this gift. But because Cassandra refused to be his lover, he also cursed her. While she always spoke the truth, Apollo made sure no one ever believed her.

continued

Did Helen fall in love with Paris and agree to elope with him? Or was she kidnapped and kept a prisoner in Troy for ten years?

Neither, according to one myth. This odd version states that though Helen was kidnapped, she never made it to Troy. On the way, Paris and Helen stopped in Egypt. A king there rescued Helen and kept her safely in his country for ten years. Finally, at the end of the war, her husband retrieved her.

Meanwhile, Paris continued on to Troy with a phantom Helen. So the great Trojan War wasn't even fought over a real woman!

The story above is also said to explain Homer's blindness. Legends say that Homer was the poet who put *The Iliad*—the story of the Trojan War—into final form. In Homer's version, Helen willingly goes with Paris to Troy. Some Greeks who argued that she had been kidnapped said Homer was struck blind for this lie.

ORPHEUS AND EURYDICE

VOCABULARY PREVIEW

Below is a list of words that appear in the story. Read the list and get to know the words before you start the story.

captivated—charmed; fascinated
compelling—forceful; persuasive; moving
console—comfort; cheer up
decreed—ordered; ruled
doom—death or fate
irrational—unreasonable; crazy
irresistible—tempting; overpowering
mesmerized—hypnotized; entranced
mourned—felt sorrow; cried over
omen—sign; warning
reprieved—given relief
reverie—daydream
riddled—pierced
shun—avoid; deliberately ignore
slither—glide; slip and slide
spite—offend; irritate
surly—unfriendly; grouchy
treacherous—dangerous; unsafe
vile—disgusting; unpleasant
woeful—sad; heartbreaking

ORPHEUS
and
EURYDICE

*How far would you go
to save someone you loved?
To hell and back?
That's the choice the young husband
in this story faces.
Yet while he may conquer his fear,
he can't conquer something
more likely to defeat him:
his undying love.*

On a hillside in Thrace,
Orpheus sang happily to the
world.[1]

*Sing streams! My bride approaches.
Sing hills! Shake out your folds.
Sing woods! Dance for my lady.
Sing sun! Spread your robe of gold.
Sing all! Eurydice[2] is mine!*

[1](thrās) (or′ fūs or or′ fē us)
[2](ū rid′ i sē)

As he sang, the trees lifted up their branches to hear him. A clear stream bubbled up in response. All the wild animals nearby stopped to listen.

Orpheus was famous for his charming music and enchanting voice. It is no surprise that he developed such talents. His goddess mother, Calliope,[3] was the guardian of poetry. She was also known for her lovely voice.

Orpheus' father was Oeagrus,[4] king of Thrace. But some people hinted that he was really the son of Apollo,[5] the god of music and poetry. In any case, the great Apollo gave the infant Orpheus a splendid lyre.[6]

As Orpheus grew, he learned to sing and play wonderful melodies. In fact, every person, animal, and thing in nature loved him for his music. No wonder the nymph[7] Eurydice fell in love with him. And Orpheus found Eurydice just as **irresistible**. She was so beautiful, kind, and faithful. It wasn't long before they set a date for their wedding.

The day of the joyful event arrived. A huge crowd gathered to witness the wedding. Everywhere, a sweet odor of incense and flowers filled the air.

After the ceremony, the wedding feast began. The beaming groom and bride moved among the guests, trading happy words.

Then Orpheus noticed Hymen,[8] the god of marriage, standing apart from the crowd. "Eurydice," said Orpheus, "Hymen is here. Shall we greet him?"

Eurydice stared at the god. "He doesn't look happy, my love. Maybe we should leave him alone."

"Of course not!" exclaimed Orpheus. "It would be bad manners for us to **shun** him. He might be angry if we avoided him."

---

[3](ka lī' ō pē)
[4](ē' a grus)
[5](a pol' lō)
[6]A lyre is a small, hand-held harp.
[7](nimpf) A nymph is a female spirit that can take many forms, including human form. Nymphs live in the forests and waters.
[8](hī' men)

So hand in hand, the newlyweds approached the god. As they drew closer, Hymen held up his bridal torch. The glare startled the couple, but they did not turn away. Still, they gripped each other's hands more tightly.

"Greetings, wise god," Orpheus said respectfully.

"What blessings have you brought us?" Eurydice asked as cheerfully as she could. Yet she suspected something was wrong.

The god said nothing. Instead, he stared at the couple with a hopeless look.

Suddenly Hymen's torch began smoking. It filled the air with a burning cloud, bringing tears to the couple's eyes.

Then Hymen spoke. "I am sorry to bring you this unlucky **omen**. I fear it means your time together on earth will last but a brief moment."

The god waved his torch and then disappeared.

Eurydice gazed sadly at her husband. In her heart, she felt that the god's warning was true.

Orpheus guessed what Eurydice was feeling. Softly he stroked her hair and tried to **console** her.

"The god must be mistaken," he said. "And if he is not, I will ask the great Apollo for help. Besides, our love is strong. We can overcome any tragedy."

"Perhaps you are right," Eurydice said as calmly as possible. "Well, for now, let's put all sad thoughts aside. Our friends are waiting."

Eurydice said these words bravely, but she didn't really believe them. She felt certain Hymen's prophecy would come to pass.

The newlyweds returned to the feast. They received many blessings from their guests. Then the wine flowed, and everyone celebrated loudly. With all the merriment, the couple seemed to forget the god's words.

In the following days, neither Orpheus nor Eurydice mentioned the omen. In fact, Orpheus did not ask Apollo for help. But just as Hymen predicted, tragedy struck.

It happened one day not long after the wedding. Eurydice

was walking in the meadows near her home. Aristaeus,[9] son of a water nymph, was also out in the meadows. He was tending a herd of cattle when he spied Eurydice.

Aristaeus stared in wonder at Eurydice. Her beauty left him breathless. He was **captivated** by her graceful movements as she stepped lightly with bare feet.

"Such beauty!" Aristaeus exclaimed. "She must be mine!" He immediately ran after Eurydice.

Eurydice heard the noise behind her and turned. When she saw a man following, panic seized her. At once she fled for home.

The graceful Eurydice quickly left Aristaeus behind. But in her fright, she forgot that her feet were bare. She did not remember to look where she ran.

Even as Eurydice neared home, she felt a painful sting on one foot. When she looked down, she gasped. On the ground, she saw a dreadful snake **slither** away.

The poison from the snake's bite quickly spread through poor Eurydice's body. Too weak even to walk, she slumped among the flowers. "Orpheus, my love," she whispered. Then death took her.

Evening came, and Orpheus grew worried about Eurydice's long absence. He set out to search for his wife. All too soon he discovered her lifeless body in the meadows.

Orpheus was overcome with grief. He brought his wife's body home and **mourned** for days. No one could console him. Even at Eurydice's funeral, Orpheus hardly spoke to his friends who offered support. Instead, he let his lyre speak for him. He played a hauntingly sad song that brought everyone to tears.

But after the funeral, Orpheus put his lyre away and refused to play. For a long time, he suffered in miserable silence. He even thought of taking his own life. Yet how could he be sure that in death he would rejoin his beloved Eurydice?

Then one day, a thought struck him. "I'll go to the Under-

[9](ar is tē' us)

world!'' he cried out. "I'll bring Eurydice back!"

Orpheus decided to set out at once. He was determined to see the king and queen of the Lower Regions. Surely Pluto and his wife Proserpina would return Eurydice to him.[10] Even the mightiest of gods respected the power of love.

Before starting out the door, Orpheus paused. Then he turned to a small chest and drew out his lyre. Orpheus well knew how dangerous his journey would be. Even a sword would probably be useless. But the power of his music could tame every creature on earth. Perhaps it would serve him in the Underworld as well.

The descent to the Lower Regions was terrifying. Orpheus entered a cave and made his way down a dark, gloomy passage. At the end of the passage stood the great, heavy gates of the Underworld. There a fierce, three-headed dog stood guard. From his mouth flowed a **vile**, black liquid. Cerberus![11]

Orpheus knew he would be attacked if he did not take quick action. The only thing he could think to do was to play a soothing song. So he took up his lyre and plucked it softly.

The tune quickly **mesmerized** the dog-monster. He relaxed and lay down to rest.

"Good night, pup," Orpheus said. He patted Cerberus on the back and hurriedly entered the gates of Pluto's kingdom.

Soon Orpheus found himself at the edge of a misty river. On the bank stood dozens of moaning and wailing souls.

"Charon,[12] won't you take me now!" one soul cried.

"Help me, Charon. Let me join my family on the other side!" another soul pleaded.

Orpheus turned and looked in the direction they were shouting. He saw an old man in a boat come into view on the river.

---

[10](plū' tō) (pro ser' pi na)
[11](ser' ber us)
[12](ka' ron)

"So this is Charon," thought Orpheus. "So this is the famous ferryman who took spirits across the river, deeper into the Underworld."

"Fools! You know I cannot take you yet!" Charon yelled. Indeed, he could not. These poor souls had not been properly buried. So each had to wait a hundred years before crossing. Such was the law Pluto had **decreed**.

With his strong voice, Orpheus managed to make his own words heard. "But you will take *me* now, Charon," he said boldly. "I am the son of a goddess. I come from the land of the living to see Pluto and Proserpina."

"I have no duty to take you!" Charon shouted back. "You people from earth come here too often, asking too much. Now I have work to do. I must take across the souls who rightfully belong in the Underworld. Go back to your home! You'll return here soon enough, anyway, mortal. For once and for all."

"Perhaps so. But I still wish to cross," replied Orpheus. "Perhaps if I paid you with a tune?"

At that, Orpheus took out his lyre and played an enchanting melody. For a moment, the poor souls on the bank forgot their sorrow. Even Charon's heart melted. The **surly** old man took Orpheus across the river without another protest.

"Thank you, old man," Orpheus said when they reached the shore. "I shall always remember this."

"You are quite welcome. Good luck on your quest," Charon replied.

Orpheus hurried on deeper into the land of the dead. Though he had heard rumors of the mysteries here, he was still astonished. In a place called the Elysian[13] Fields, he found a glorious paradise. Orpheus anxiously peered through the gates, searching for Eurydice among those happy souls. But he couldn't spot her there.

As Orpheus continued on his way, some terrible cries came to his ears. Ah, he could guess who those unhappy

[13](e lizh′ i an)

souls were! He knew they must be the damned. These mortals and gods had committed crimes or foolishly angered the gods. They were all now confined in Tartarus,[14] the blackest place in the Lower Regions.

As he passed this place of horror, Orpheus saw Tantalus.[15] This evil king had committed several crimes to **spite** the gods. He had even dared kill his own son and serve the boy's flesh to the Olympians.[16]

Now Tantalus stood in a lake of water, surrounded by trees of tempting fruit. Yet whenever he tried to pick some fruit, the branches pulled away. And when he bent down to drink water, a wave drew it back. The miserable man looked sadly at Orpheus as he passed by.

Orpheus next came to a hill where he saw Sisyphus.[17] This crafty man had stolen, raped, and murdered. He'd also insulted and betrayed the gods. For these crimes, he was sentenced to roll a heavy stone up a hill over and over again.

Another mortal who murdered and schemed against the gods was King Ixion. Ixion foolishly tried to rape Juno, queen of the gods.[18] His punishment was to be tied to an endlessly spinning wheel and whipped with snakes.

Orpheus also saw the Danaids.[19] He knew the story of these forty-nine sisters, who had all married on the same day. These hard-hearted women had then murdered their husbands that night.

In the Underworld, the sisters were punished by having to carry water in jars **riddled** with holes. Theirs was an endless task since the water ran out as fast as the jars were filled.

Orpheus finally arrived at the throne of King Pluto and Queen Proserpina.

---

[14](tar' tar us)
[15](tan' ta lus)
[16](ō lim' pi anz) The twelve major Greek gods were known as the Olympians after the place where many of them lived: Mt. Olympus.
[17](sis' i fus)
[18](ik sī' on) (jū' nō)
[19](dan' ā idz)

"Please, my king and queen," Orpheus addressed the astonished pair. "Please listen to me. My name is Orpheus and this is my story."

With that he played a **woeful** song about Eurydice's death and his own suffering.

O mighty gods of the Underworld,
We mortals live on earth but a day.
Yet even that fleeting moment grows long
When loved ones are taken away.

Dear gods, my Eurydice left the cup untouched.
The sweet bud was cut before she bloomed.
Now I sleep, between tears and sighs,
*Dreaming of my love and her cruel **doom**.*

King Pluto, you know the pain of longing
When fair Prosperina leaves your side.[20]
So return my bride to me for a while.
Bathe my wounded heart in a joyous tide.

As Orpheus sang, some wonderful things happened. The Danaids paused to listen, and the water in their jars stopped flowing. Ixion's wheel ground to a halt. Sisyphus' stone stopped rolling. For the first time in years he rested. Tantalus, too, was **reprieved**. The water in the lake stood still at long last, allowing him to drink. Even the Furies, the goddesses of revenge, wept for Orpheus.

Orpheus' song also touched the hearts of Pluto and Proserpina. "Your song is **compelling**," mighty Pluto said. "I cannot ignore such suffering, my friend. Eurydice is yours."

Orpheus could hardly believe what he was hearing. His sadness gave way to joy. But as he sprang forward to bless the god, Pluto held up a hand.

---

[20] Proserpina remained in the Lower Regions only part of the year. Her return to the upper world every year marked the beginning of spring. Her departure for the Underworld, on the other hand, signaled the start of winter.

"Eurydice is yours, but only under one condition," the god warned. "You may look once at her here. Then you must not look at her again until you lead her into the upper world. Do you think you can do this?"

"Oh yes, of course!" Orpheus agreed.

Eurydice was soon brought to Orpheus. The two lovers embraced and thanked the rulers of the Underworld. Then they set out on their journey to earth. Eurydice silently followed her faithful husband. Both were too overjoyed for words. They had actually overcome Hymen's prophecy!

They quickly passed Tartarus and the Elysian Fields. Once at the river, Charon ferried them across without any protests. Orpheus was careful to sit in the front of the boat, while Eurydice sat at the back. In this way, he could not see his bride.

At the gates of Pluto's kingdom, Orpheus played his lyre for Cerberus. The dog-monster cheerfully let the happy couple pass.

Orpheus thought, "We only need to travel the dark passage up to earth now." His heart was bursting with gladness. In silence, he and Eurydice made their way through the **treacherous** tunnel.

Finally a ray of light from the earth shone on Orpheus. "At last!" he thought. "At last my wife and I will be together in the land of the living!" Then he stepped into the upper world.

Orpheus turned to take Eurydice's hand. Alas, in his eagerness, he forgot Pluto's words. For Eurydice was still in the passage and had not yet set foot on earth.

Orpheus immediately saw his mistake. "What have I done?" he cried.

Eurydice knew the sad answer to that. Lovingly, she held out her arms. Oh, if she could just hold her dear husband one last time! But she only grasped the air.

"Goodbye, my Orpheus. I'll always love you," Eurydice called out. But Orpheus barely heard her call his name. Already her spirit was being pulled back to the Underworld.

To the skies, Orpheus shouted, "No! Please, it can't be! Give me another chance!"

He turned and rushed back down the dark passage, straight back to the gates. This time, though, he could not get through. Cerberus threatened to attack him, his three vicious heads snapping at once. The dog would not be calmed, even though Orpheus played his lyre.

For seven days Orpheus tried to persuade the gods to let him pass through the gates. But they would not listen.

At last poor Orpheus returned to his home in Thrace. Day after day, he grieved. No one heard the sound of his lovely voice or lyre. He simply sat, mourning his dead wife. He knew he could never love another woman.

However, there were many women in Thrace who were attracted to Orpheus. Now that he had no wife, some of them hoped to marry him.

One of those who loved Orpheus was a Bacchante. The Bacchantes were female followers of Bacchus, the god of wine.[21] They worshipped the god by drinking so much wine that they became crazy.

The Bacchante who loved Orpheus was determined to have him. She thought time would heal Orpheus' grief and make him ready to love again. "One day he will be mine!" she told another follower.

The Bacchante's chance came one day when Orpheus went to the hillsides. Orpheus took his lyre because he thought he might make music once again. When he came to a lovely spot, he sat down and thought of Eurydice. Before he knew it, he was playing a song for her.

Suddenly his song was interrupted by loud noises. Orpheus turned and saw a group of drunken Bacchantes dancing wildly nearby. Among them was the lovestruck Bacchante. And it wasn't long before she spied Orpheus.

She rushed at him madly. "At last, my love! I have waited weeks for you to appear," she shouted.

Orpheus was startled by this horrid, drunken woman. She

[21](bak′ kan tē) (bak′ kus)

stank from too much wine.

"Please," Orpheus begged. "Respect my grief. Leave me alone with my thoughts."

"Your thoughts!" the woman shouted. "All you ever think of is your dead wife. But I can make you forget her," she said, grasping his arms.

Orpheus moved away. "Never! Until my dying days, she shall be the only woman for me. Now leave," Orpheus said firmly.

The woman became quite angry. And because she was drunk, she was very **irrational**. "You'll pay for this insult!" she hissed. Then she rushed away.

Orpheus was rid of her. Or at least so he believed. His thoughts drifted back to Eurydice. Again he began to play a song for her. Soon he was deep in **reverie**, happily playing his music. That is why he never noticed the Bacchante return with her friends until too late.

Under the angry Bacchante's directions, the women gathered in a circle. Then they began throwing spears and stones at Orpheus. But none of these missiles hurt Orpheus because his music protected him. The objects simply fell harmlessly around him.

The Bacchantes began to curse and scream angrily. "Who do you think you are?" yelled one.

"You cannot insult our sister like this!" shouted another. "You think you're quite a catch. But you're nothing!" called another.

Now their cries drowned out Orpheus' music. And the stones they threw began to hit him. Soon he was weak and bloody.

"O gods, save me from these mad women!" Orpheus gasped.

But it was too late. The savage Bacchantes closed in on Orpheus and tore his limbs from his body. Then they cut off his head and threw it, along with his lyre, into the river. From there, the head and lyre were carried to the island of

Lesbos.[22] The Bacchantes also scattered his limbs and body in the hills near Thrace.

The Muses,[23] goddesses of the arts, soon heard of this tragic event. To honor the great musician, they rescued his lyre and placed it among the stars. To this day, it still shines brightly there.

Next, the Muses gathered Orpheus' body parts. Then they took him to Mount Olympus, home of the gods, for burial. There a nightingale is said to sing sweetly over his grave.

From such a shocking and sad end came happiness. Because the Muses had buried him properly, Orpheus' spirit was quickly admitted to see Pluto.

"Orpheus, you have been a faithful husband," the king said. "Now you and Eurydice shall be reunited forever in paradise."

As before, Eurydice was brought to Orpheus. They clung to each other, and Eurydice spoke. "My love, I knew you would return soon. Let us go now to the Elysian Fields."

So together, the lovers entered paradise. And there they will remain forever.

[22](les' bos)
[23](mūz' ez)

INSIGHTS

The myth of Orpheus and Eurydice is clearly from the Greeks. However, no Greek versions of the myth exist. Some of the first recorded versions are from the great Roman poets Ovid and Virgil.

But since its first appearance, the myth has been retold many times by artists. It has been especially popular in opera. Interestingly enough, many of these operas end happily. One—Offenbach's *Orpheus in the Underworld*—even treats the whole story in a comic way.

The Orpheus myth has also served as the subject for plays and movies. Tennessee Williams' version, *Orpheus Descending,* has been staged and filmed. A more strange production is Cocteau's *Orpheus.* This retelling features a motorcycle gang, a mysterious lady in black, and a mirror that is a doorway to Hell.

At one time, Orpheus became the center of a religious cult. In this cult, which lasted until the fourth century A.D., Orpheus served as a savior. In the form of a fisherman, he used a fishing line to take people on a trip through water. The trip helped awaken a person's mind and spirit. T.S. Eliot built his famous poem "The Waste Land" around this legend of Orpheus.

The religious cult still survives—in our vocabulary. The word *orphic* now means *mystical.*

continued

Orpheus was one of those who sailed with Jason to fetch the Golden Fleece. On the journey, Orpheus' music relaxed the crew when they grew tired. His music also soothed them when they quarreled.

Orpheus' music was even powerful enough to defeat the deadly Sirens. The singing of these creatures lured many to crash their ships against the rocks. But Jason's ship passed safely because Orpheus' music was more powerful than their voices.

The Elysian Fields is the place in the Underworld where Orpheus and Eurydice are reunited. Now the name refers to any place of great joy. *Champs Elysees,* a famous street in Paris, is a fine example of a modern Elysian Field.

And what of Aristaeus, the "villain"? Aristaeus did pay for his part in Eurydice's death. This son of Apollo was a beekeeper. So Eurydice's fellow nymphs struck back at him by killing all his bees.

After seeking out a prophet, Aristaeus learned why his bees had died. He also learned that to make up for the crime, he must sacrifice some animals to the gods. Then he was to wait nine days.

Aristaeus did all this. And when he returned to the place of sacrifice, he found he'd been forgiven. For a new swarm of bees was buzzing about the dead animals.

Artistaeus was later worshipped as a god of shepherds and, of course, bees.

OEDIPUS

VOCABULARY PREVIEW

Below is a list of words that appear in the story. Read the list and get to know the words before you start the story.

apprehension—worry; fear
ashen—very pale; ghostly
awestruck—struck speechless; amazed
banished—exiled; sent out of the country
brooches—decorative pins
brutality—cruelty
corpses—dead bodies
desolate—deserted; empty
devours—gulps; eats quickly
fork—place where a road divides
plague—deadly disease that spreads quickly
pronouncement—public announcement
pulsed—beat or throbbed
reconcile—make peace; reunite
regal—royal; like a ruler
scepter—ruler's staff or wand
torment—torture
torso—trunk of the human body
trek—journey; trip
unwittingly—unknowingly; accidentally

OEDIPUS

> **"Who am I?"**
>
> *On the surface, that may not seem like a very deep riddle. For master-riddler Oedipus, however, that question—and its answer—is the toughest he'll ever face.*

from SOPHOCLES' OEDIPUS TRILOGY

Oedipus[1] stood at a **fork** in the road. "Which way do I turn?" he wondered. "Which way to the nearest city? It's a riddle, surely! How can I answer it?"

Young Oedipus was not a patient man. And now his patience was at an end. He bent down to rub his feet. They were sore from long walking. For as long as he could remember, they had caused him pain. That is how he had gotten his name, which meant "swollen foot."

[1](ē′ di pus or e′ di pus)

A sound in the distance drew Oedipus' attention back to the road. He listened carefully. It was the sound of hoofs. Now he noticed a cloud of dust on the road to the left.

After several minutes, a guard rode up on a fine horse. Behind the guard rolled a magnificent chariot, circled by three other horsemen. In the chariot, beside the driver, stood a **regal** man. Though he seemed quite old, he stood as tall and strong as the mast of a ship.

"Out of our way!" the guard barked at Oedipus. He raised his sword threateningly.

"Gladly," replied Oedipus, trying to keep his temper. "But first, please tell me which road leads to the nearest city."

"None—if you don't move this instant!" said the guard.

The old man in the chariot rose to his feet. "Guard!" he yelled. "What's holding us up?"

"Some stubborn young rascal blocking our way," replied the guard.

"Let me talk to him," shouted the old man.

The guard moved aside. Oedipus strode toward the chariot.

"And now tell me, bold idiot," said the old man. "What makes you, a mere wanderer, decide to stop my chariot?"

Oedipus looked into the man's eyes. They were filled with all the fury of a summer storm. Clearly, this fellow was just as impatient as Oedipus. It was not good for two such short-tempered men to cross paths. Oedipus knew that, but nothing could be done now.

"I was just asking a question," replied Oedipus. I only wanted to know which road to take."

"A question!" roared the old man. "You stop my chariot for a stupid question! Why, boy, do you have any idea who I am?"

"No idea at all," said Oedipus, burning with rage. "Nor do I care."

The old man's face bloomed a rose red. He raised himself to his full height and swung his **scepter** at Oedipus.

The old man was strong, but Oedipus was stronger. Oedipus grabbed the scepter and pulled it hard. Thrown off his balance, the man tumbled from the chariot.

At once he tried to raise himself from the ground. But Oedipus struck him again with the scepter. The man fell dead at his feet.

Instantly the first guard rode at Oedipus, sword flashing. Oedipus pulled the man from his horse and killed him, too. Then wild with rage, he killed three of the others.

When his killing fever cooled, Oedipus stepped back. He gazed at the **corpses** at his feet. For a moment, he thought he had killed them all. But then he heard the clatter of hoofs. He looked up to see one horseman riding away.

"Go on!" yelled Oedipus. "Run like the coward you are! And tell your people not to cross me again!"

Oedipus sank down to the ground, wearier than ever.

"Why?" he wondered. "Why did I let myself do it? Could I have defended myself without killing them?"

After thinking for a long moment, Oedipus decided. "No. There were too many of them. I had no choice."

The only thing to do was to get up and move along. He chose the road the chariot had come from and plodded on.

As Oedipus walked, he thought and remembered. The terrible events of the last few days came back to him. It hadn't been more than a week since he had left Corinth.[2]

Ah, Corinth! Oedipus had been happy there. In fact, he had been a prince, the son of King Polybus and Queen Merope.[3]

But at a banquet, his life had suddenly changed. At that feast, a drunken man told Oedipus he was not really Polybus' son. Furious, Oedipus grabbed the man and vowed to kill him. But something in the drunkard's eyes made Oedipus believe the story.

So that night, Oedipus questioned his father and mother. They laughed at the gossip. They swore that Oedipus was really their son.

[2](kor' inth)
[3](pol' i bus) (mer' ō pē)

Yet Oedipus thought they seemed uneasy. He suspected that the whole truth was still to be discovered. At the same time, he was fearful. A sailor who finds that his ship is less sturdy than he believed learns a valuable lesson. Yet the cost of that knowledge might be high indeed. Would the truth drown Oedipus?

However, Oedipus had never turned away from uncovering the truth. So without telling a soul, he left for the Delphic Oracle next morning.[4] There those who dared could hear the future foretold.

As Oedipus suspected, the priestess of the temple revealed some deep secrets. And the news was horrifying. "You are doomed to kill your father," the priestess told him. "What's more, you shall live in sin with your mother. You shall have children by her."

Stunned, Oedipus stumbled away. He fled deep into the hills and finally fell to his knees. "To kill my father!" he cried. "And to wed my own mother! How could I ever do such things?"

Oedipus knew the oracle always spoke truthfully. He also had heard that no one could escape the prophecies.

But he had to try. He couldn't go back to Corinth. He must leave Polybus and Merope behind forever. He would even forget his princedom. Surely with all these sacrifices, he could stop the prophecy from coming true.

Once he'd reached his decision, Oedipus had set off on his wandering. Since then he'd been on the road for days, fleeing from crimes. And now he had just slain five men. He hoped the future would demand less **brutality**.

With his memories for company, Oedipus made good time down the road he'd chosen. By the next morning, he reached a city. He knew at once from the seven gates that this must be Thebes.[5] Oedipus had heard strange and wonderful tales of this place. But to him it had always seemed like the

---

[4](del' fic) An oracle is a person or thing that is a source of wisdom and truth. The oracle at Delphi, sacred to the god Apollo, was the most famous oracle in Greece.
[5](thēbz)

rainbow—ever distant and not quite real.

Now Oedipus found Thebes' great gates closed. He called out to a guard atop one gate.

"Greetings!" he cried. "Can't anyone come in?"

"No one," said the guard. "The city is completely closed off. You've been on the road, have you?"

"Yes," said Oedipus. "For some days now. I'm anxious to rest."

"And you haven't met up with the Sphinx?"[6]

"I don't even know what a sphinx is," replied Oedipus.

"She's a monster who **devours** anyone that strays near," the guard explained. "She's brought terrible hardship on this city. We don't dare open the gates for fear that she would attack." The guard sighed. "As if we hadn't troubles enough. Our old king was just killed."

"So you have no leader?" Oedipus asked.

"Oh, we have a leader. Creon,[7] brother of the king's widow, has stepped in. But he's willing to step back down again—for the right man."

"The right man?"

"The one who kills the Sphinx."

Oedipus turned away thoughtfully. "A monster for a throne," he murmured. "Perhaps I should take a look at this Sphinx." He began walking down the road.

Oedipus hadn't long to wait. Before he had gone a few miles from Thebes, he found the Sphinx. She stood blocking the road like one of Thebes' gates.

Oedipus stared in wonder at the creature. The Sphinx had a body like a lion with wings. Her head and **torso** were those of a beautiful woman.

"You are the Sphinx, I take it," he said.

"Indeed," said the Sphinx. "And you are dust, young stranger! Food for the earth. Whispers of bone."

Oedipus looked about for a rock or stick to use as a

[6](sfinks)
[7](krē' on)

weapon. At the same time he tried to keep the Sphinx occupied with talk. "So you won't give me any chance to defend myself?" he asked.

"Only one," said the Sphinx with a smile. "A riddle. Solve it and you're free to go."

Oedipus laughed. "What?" he exclaimed. "No combat to the death? Just a mere riddle?"

"Oh, this is a deep riddle! Deeper than Tartarus,"[8] said the Sphinx. "No human has ever answered it. All of them have ended up as my meat. So do you care to attempt it?"

In spite of the danger, Oedipus was greatly amused. After all, he had been known for his intelligence since childhood. Riddles had fascinated him for years. Surely, this Sphinx didn't know a riddle he hadn't already heard.

"Gladly!" he agreed. "But tell me, what is my prize if I guess correctly?"

"The stakes are simple," said the Sphinx. "My life against yours. Agreed?"

"Agreed," said Oedipus.

The Sphinx gave a delighted grin. Then softly she spoke the riddle. "What creature walks first on four legs, then two, and finally three?"

Oedipus was taken by surprise. No, he'd never heard this riddle before.

He sat down and thought. As the minutes slipped by, the Sphinx edged closer. Sweat began to form on Oedipus' brow.

At last the answer came to him.

"Of course! It's man!" he cried. "As a baby, he crawls or walks on four legs. When he's grown, he walks on two. Then in old age he uses a cane—and that's three legs! Now, Sphinx, have I answered your riddle correctly?"

But the Sphinx couldn't speak. The monster's eyes glazed over and her body turned to stone. She crashed to the ground and broke into pieces.

Oedipus was delighted to have bested the Sphinx and won entry to Thebes. Quickly he returned to Thebes. Yet he

[8](tar' tar us) Tartarus was the deepest place in the earth. It was a place in the Underworld set aside for the torture of criminals.

didn't travel quite as quickly as some shepherds who had seen the Sphinx destroyed. They had arrived in Thebes ahead of Oedipus and spread the story. So the city gates stood open when Oedipus arrived.

As soon as Oedipus entered Thebes, the shepherds spotted him. "That's him!" they cried. "The one who killed the Sphinx!"

Soon a crowd of happy citizens had gathered round Oedipus. But suddenly the crowd parted. Creon, ruler of Thebes, stepped forward.

"Everyone here knows of my promise," he said. "And I will keep it. The throne is yours. Any man who was brave and wise enough to kill the Sphinx will make a fine king."

Oedipus had already made up his mind about the offer. This was one way to forget about his lost family and power. So he accepted and became King Oedipus, ruler of Thebes.

As king, Oedipus married the dead king's widow, Jocasta.[9] She was much older than he was but still beautiful. He was pleased to take her as his bride.

Oedipus ruled Thebes wisely for many years. And he and Jocasta were very happy with one another. They had four children together. Two of these were daughters, Antigone and Ismene.[10] The other two were sons, Polynices and Eteocles.[11] It was a fine family, the envy of people far and near.

But one day, a new crisis struck Thebes. A terrible **plague** came, killing people, animals, and crops. The streets were littered with the dead. Funeral songs and weeping filled the air. Those who were left alive faced hardship and starvation.

Oedipus was heartbroken by the woe of his adopted home. So he made a bold decision. Once before he had gone to the Delphic Oracle for help. Now he would send his brother-in-law, Creon, to ask for advice.

Creon soon completed his journey and brought back the oracle's **pronouncement**. There was only one way to stop

[9] (jō kas' ta)
[10] (an tig' o nē) (is mē' nē)
[11] (pol i nī' sēz) (e tē' o klēz)

the plague, it said. The Thebans must find the murderer of Laius[12] and drive him out of the city.

Oedipus was pleased. As a solver of riddles, surely he could find Laius' murderer.

He went before the people of Thebes and told them the news. "We must find the killer of Laius," he said. "I need the help of every one of you. But understand this. No mercy will be shown to the murderer's protectors. If you know who he is or where he lives, come forward! I will hold even myself to this command. If the murderer lives in my own household, I'll bring him to justice. Or else I vow to suffer the punishment myself!"

Then Oedipus sent for the blind prophet Teiresias.[13] For many years, Teiresias had spoken wisely to the Thebans. Oedipus now hoped the prophet would offer clues about the murderer.

But when Teiresias arrived, he listened in silence to Oedipus' request. Not one word would he say.

Oedipus felt his patience slipping like a greased rope from his fingers. Why was this fellow being so stubborn?

"What's the matter, old man?" he asked. "Surely you can't be speechless for the first time in your life!"

"Not speechless," Teiresias coldly replied. "I just don't think you'll like my words."

"Tell me!" demanded Oedipus. "Or I'll punish you as if you were the murderer himself!"

A strange expression crossed Teiresias' face. It was both bitter and puzzled. Oedipus could see that Teiresias, too, was short of temper.

"Very well," Teiresias said. "Though not much welcome you'll give my news. You, yourself, are the murderer you seek!"

Oedipus' blood boiled with fury. He rose from his throne.

"Liar!" he cried. "You and I both know that's not true! Surely you don't expect these people to believe your words.

[12](lā′ us)
[13](ti rē′ si as)

It doesn't take much skill with riddles to see through you. Someone's paid you well to accuse me. Why, I wouldn't be surprised if you didn't kill Laius yourself!"

The people were shocked to hear Oedipus say such things. Teiresias was a holy man. No one had ever dared show him disrespect.

But a smile played across Teiresias' lips. "You seem so fortunate, Oedipus," he said. "Everyone envies your wisdom and your power. But you are really most unfortunate. Why, you don't even know who you are!"

With that, the old man turned and left.

Oedipus' mind filled with confusion. Surely, Teiresias was part of some plot. Why else would he tell such horrible lies? And yet the old man seemed quite sincere. This was the most difficult riddle Oedipus had ever untangled.

Oedipus decided to seek out Jocasta. His wife often gave him good advice.

Jocasta calmly listened to Oedipus' story. When he finished, she startled him by laughing.

"What did you expect, dear husband?" she said. "Oracles and prophets know nothing. It's all just superstition. To prove it, let me tell you a story. Laius and I had only one child, a son. Laius went to the Delphic Oracle to learn the boy's fate. Poor Laius hoped for some glorious prophecy. But the priestess revealed that the boy would someday kill him!

"Well, I didn't believe it. But Laius did. He had the baby's feet fastened together. The poor child was in awful pain, and his feet swelled terribly. Then Laius gave the baby to one of our servants. He gave orders that the baby was to be left on a nearby mountain. And as Laius commanded, the deed was done."

Jocasta shook her head and sighed. "The child could not have lived long. The mountain is cold and **desolate**."

She paused as she let the memories sift through her mind. "Poor Laius. He met an unhappy death anyway. To be murdered—and so far from home. I wonder if he saw his

death coming as he stood there? What a lonely place to die!
A dusty crossroads where three roads meet.''

Jocasta sighed again. ''Well, at any rate, it proves the
oracle was wrong—as always!''

But instead of being relieved, Oedipus was startled by
Jocasta's words. ''You said that Laius was killed at a place
where three roads meet?''

''Why, yes,'' said Jocasta, disturbed by Oedipus' expression.

''And who was with him at the time?'' asked Oedipus.

''Five men in all. Only one got away alive.'' Jocasta
reached out a comforting hand. ''Oedipus, what is it? Why
do my words trouble you?''

Oedipus trembled with **apprehension**. ''I may have done
a terrible thing,'' he said. ''If so, I can only swear I did it
without knowing.''

He told Jocasta of the men he had killed. He described
the regal man and his five companions. He explained that
the killings had happened where three roads meet.

''Surely you cannot have killed Laius!'' said Jocasta.
''This is only a coincidence.''

''But I must find out for certain!'' exclaimed Oedipus.

Oedipus sent for the man who had fled the scene of Laius'
killing. It turned out he had far to look. The man was no
longer a servant at the palace. When Oedipus was crowned,
the man had left Thebes. Now he was a shepherd in the
deepest part of the hills.

As Oedipus and Jocasta anxiously waited for the
shepherd, another man arrived. He was a messenger, bringing more startling news.

''Greetings, noble Oedipus,'' he said. ''I have come from
your home city, Corinth. I bear sad news, I fear. Polybus,
your father, is dead. But to comfort your sorrow, I bring
good news as well. The people want you to return and be
their king.''

''Polybus dead?'' Tears misted Oedipus' eyes. Then he
quickly asked, ''But my mother? Is Merope still alive?''

"Alive and well," said the messenger.

"Good news. Yet it means that I cannot come with you," replied Oedipus. He explained to the messenger why he had fled Corinth. He told him of the prophecy. True, part of the prophecy had not come to pass. Oedipus had not killed Polybus.

But what about Merope? Oedipus dreaded the other half of the prophecy.

The messenger laughed at this. "Is that what worries you?" he asked. "Is that why you've been gone from Corinth all these years? Why, you're no more Polybus' son than I am! You were adopted! And I, myself, gave you to Polybus and Merope.

"You see, I was once a shepherd in these parts. One day I met a man carrying a tiny baby. He said he was a servant of Laius. He was about to leave the poor babe on the slopes to die. But I took the baby to Corinth. I gave him to the king and queen. And you were that baby."

"But whose child am I?" cried Oedipus. He was thrilled at the thought of learning his identity.

"I have no idea," admitted the messenger.

However, Jocasta had turned **ashen**. "Don't ask any more questions, Oedipus!" she exclaimed. "I beg you not to!"

"What could be more wonderful than to learn who I am?" asked Oedipus.

"I promise you, nothing could be more horrible!" cried Jocasta. "For your own sake, I hope you never learn the truth!"

She ran madly into the palace. Oedipus stood in stunned silence. What did her words mean? He could feel part of the riddle unraveling.

At that moment, the old shepherd arrived. He looked cautious and apprehensive.

The messenger from Corinth let loose a yelp of surprise. "But this is the very man!" he said. "He was the one who gave you to me!"

"Be quiet, you fool!" said the shepherd. "I've never seen

you before in my life."

"Why are you lying?" asked the messenger. "Why, I'd recognize you anywhere!"

Oedipus was seized with a terrible realization. He knew he was about to learn a dreadful truth. Yet he couldn't turn back from it now.

Oedipus grabbed the shepherd by the arm. "Tell me!" he commanded. "Are you who this messenger says you are?"

"Yes!" groaned the shepherd through his tears.

"And whose child am I?"

The shepherd looked up at Oedipus. His eyes were filled with terror and pity. "The child of Laius and Jocasta, my king!" he cried. "And may the gods have mercy on you!"

Oedipus was shattered by the truth. He gave an anguished cry that rang throughout Thebes. Then he turned and ran wildly through the palace.

At last Oedipus came to Jocasta's bedroom. He threw the doors open. The sight that greeted his eyes took his breath away. For he stood in the shadow of his wife and his mother—now dead. The poor woman had hanged herself.

"I cannot bear to look at her!" cried Oedipus. "I cannot bear to look upon my own children! The sight of the world itself is too awful to bear! Let me never see again!"

With that, Oedipus pulled the **brooches** from Jocasta's hair. Then, with another horrid cry, he drove the pins into his own eyes.

Thus Oedipus kept his promise to the citizens of Thebes. He had punished himself fully for the death of Laius. And as his eyesight vanished, so did the plague.

Oedipus' terrible discovery shook Thebes. Yet the mighty city lived on. To take Oedipus' place as ruler, Creon once again stepped forward. And Oedipus and his children stepped back.

For some years, Oedipus and his children continued to live in Thebes. But one day, Creon decided that Oedipus had to leave. The blinded Oedipus brought painful memories to all who saw him. He was too great a shame to the city to remain there.

So Oedipus was forced to leave Thebes. His deeply loyal daughter, Antigone, traveled with him. From city to city they roamed because no one would take them in. For years they remained homeless.

One day on their lonely **trek**, Oedipus and Antigone found themselves in a lovely wooded area. This place was called Colonus, and it was just outside of Athens.[14]

Oedipus sat down on a stone. He was overwhelmed by a strange feeling.

"Dear daughter," he said to Antigone. "The gods have told me my life will end remarkably. And I believe them."

Antigone knelt beside him and held his hand. "So do I, Father," she said.

"That day is coming. I'm certain I was meant to die here. Now, at last, I can be at peace."

The quiet moment was abruptly ruined. A man who was passing by spied them. He stopped and cried out angrily, "Get out, you two! This is a holy place! No one is allowed here!"

"What gods are sacred here?" asked Oedipus.

"The Eumenides,"[15] said the man. "Now go at once!"

"Don't be concerned," said Oedipus. "My name is Oedipus. I know that name is horrible to you. But I bring a blessing to this place. Go tell your king I wish to speak with him."

The man fled in fear. Oedipus' name had become dreadful to all who heard it.

"Yes, this is the place," said Oedipus to Antigone. "The very place I have searched for. The Eumenides shall grant me mercy here. I shall stay and await my fate."

Yet stubborn fate was not immediately kind to Oedipus. For at that moment, Oedipus' other daughter, Ismene, arrived. She brought terrible news from Thebes.

[14](ko lō′ nus) (ath′ enz)
[15](ū men′ i dēz) The Eumenides were goddesses of mercy and kindness.

"Oh, Father," she cried, "Thebes is at war! Polynices and Eteocles are fighting for the kingship. Eteocles now sits on the throne. But Polynices has gathered an army. He's about to attack the city!"

"Selfish, evil sons!" muttered Oedipus. "But what has this to do with me?"

"Uncle Creon and Eteocles want you back. An oracle has told them that they need you. Without you, their cause is lost!"

"Of course!" laughed Oedipus. "First they drive me from the city. Now they say they want me back. They say they need me."

A spark of old anger lit Oedipus' eyes. "No, my child," he declared. "I shall stay here. This is where I shall die."

"But Uncle Creon is coming!" cried Ismene. "I'm afraid he'll take you by force."

"He can do no such thing," said Oedipus. "The gods have already decided what's to become of me. Come, children, pray with me." So Oedipus and his daughters knelt and prayed to the Eumenides.

After a time, the man who had passed by returned. With him was the king of Athens—Theseus[16]—plus several guards.

Theseus was **awestruck** by the sight of the blind old man. "Oedipus!" he cried. "Then it *is* really you! I'd not have believed it if I hadn't seen you for myself. But what brings you to this sacred place? And do you mean my city well or ill?"

"Oh, King Theseus, I mean you very well!" said Oedipus. "I bring you wonderful fortune! The gods have told me so. Wretched Thebes, from which I was **banished**, will be cursed. The Thebans will suffer for their cruelty to me. But the place of my death—this very place—will be blessed. Athens will someday fight a battle here and win."

Theseus was moved by Oedipus' words. "I believe you, Oedipus," he said. "And I declare you to be a citizen of Athens."

[16](thē′ sus or thē′ sē us)

Oedipus smiled gratefully. Then he and the great king sat and talked. Oedipus told Theseus his whole story. He spoke of how he had committed his crimes **unwittingly**.

Though Theseus knew the tale, he listened in fascination. To him, Oedipus seemed like a myth come to life.

All too soon their conversation was interrupted by the arrival of Creon. With him came many soldiers. Creon approached Oedipus with a smile fixed like a mask on his face.

"Oedipus, old friend," he said. "There have been so many misunderstandings between us. But you are still family, after all. I am ready to **reconcile**. Come back to Thebes. You will be welcome there again."

"How very generous of you, Creon!" said Oedipus bitterly. "And I suppose you've come only out of good will. Strange. Why should you decide to be kind to me now?"

Creon frowned. "I take it you know about the oracle," he said. "Very well, then. If you love Thebes, you'll come and save your city."

"I do *not* love Thebes," snapped Oedipus. "In fact, I curse it forever."

Creon glared and then turned to his soldiers. "Seize the old man," he ordered. "And bring his daughters as well."

At this, Theseus stepped forward. "I rule here," he said. "You have no right to take anyone by force."

Though the frown remained on his face, Creon made a coldly polite bow. "Of course, Theseus," he said. "But do you really want this man in your midst? That poisonous snake will only hatch evil here. You know his crimes."

"And I know he committed them in innocence," replied Theseus. "There is such a thing as common courtesy. I will not turn him away."

"He is of use only to me," said Creon.

"How unfortunate for you," said Theseus. "For he is staying right here."

The two men's soldiers faced each other, ready to fight. But Creon knew he could not win against Theseus. Angry and disappointed, he led his men away.

"Thank you, Theseus," said Oedipus. "I'll not trouble you much longer. The hour of my death is near. Now I fear I keep you from your duties. You may go if you like."

"No, Oedipus. I will stay by you to the end," said Theseus.

Night approached. A storm flashed and snapped in the distance like a restless fire. As the rain rumbled closer, one last visitor appeared. It was Oedipus' son Polynices. He walked towards his father fearfully.

"I understand you have refused to return to Thebes," said Polynices.

"I have," said Oedipus.

"And you know I plan to attack the city?"

"I do."

"Father, if you come with me, we can be victorious together."

Oedipus laughed harshly. "Another one who wants my blessing, eh?" he cried. "And where was your voice when Creon banished me? Well, here's my blessing to you, Polynices. And to Eteocles as well. The two of you will soon fight hand to hand. And you will die in each other's arms, like fine, loving brothers! No, dear son," he spit back. "Ask no other blessing from me. I have none to give."

Polynices fell to his knees, weeping. His sisters wept, too, embracing him. They all knew their father's words were true.

"Please, Polynices," begged Antigone. "Don't do this thing! Don't fight against Thebes! If you do, you know you are doomed!"

But Polynices wiped her tears away. He spoke to her gently. "Dear Antigone," he said, "the gods themselves have already decided what I'll do. The choice isn't mine anymore. But do me one kindness when I die. Make sure that I'm properly buried."

Antigone nodded through her tears. With a last kiss for each sister, Polynices vanished into the night.

Suddenly the rain came pouring down. Lightning flashed right over them, splintering the sky into pieces.

Then a thunderous voice filled the heavens. "Oedipus!" it boomed. "It is time. Why do you wait so long?"

Oedipus slowly rose to his feet. He clutched Theseus' hand. "Theseus, my death is near," he whispered. "You must come with me to my final resting place. Only you may know the spot."

And so the blind old man led the young king along. He knew the way well. It was as if he had walked it every day of his life.

At last they reached the sacred place. Theseus watched as Oedipus opened his arms to the sky.

The earth itself seemed to groan. A blinding light blazed over the scene. Theseus glimpsed something extraordinary. He wasn't sure what it was. Perhaps it was the presence of some god. Or perhaps the heavens themselves had opened to receive Oedipus.

Whatever it was, Theseus found it too wondrous to look at. He closed his eyes and threw his hands across his face. Then came a huge crash of thunder and afterwards, total silence. The rain stopped.

Theseus opened his eyes. The night was now clear. The bright stars **pulsed** with the steady rhythm of a sleeper's heart.

Oedipus was gone. It was as if he had never existed.

Trembling with awe, Theseus found his way back through the grove. There he found Antigone and Ismene. The women were still weeping with grief and despair.

"Oh, tell us!" they cried. "Tell us where our father is buried."

"But he hasn't been buried," Theseus said in a voice filled with wonder. "His body has been taken by the gods themselves."

"Then show us where he died!" begged the sisters.

"I cannot," said Theseus. "Only I may know the place. But come back to Athens with me. For your father's sake, I will make sure of your safety."

Antigone took her sister's hand. "There is no safety for us," she said, drying her eyes. "Our city is at war. And I have a promise to keep to my brother."

The two sisters walked away. Theseus watched them go, his mind filled with concern. It would be a long journey back to Thebes. And great troubles waited for them there.

But he was a king, with troubles of his own. So he walked homeward, his heart heavy with wonder and confusion.

As for Oedipus, the riddle of his life was solved at last. And only he knew the answer. His life had been one long **torment**. Now for him, the torment was over. For others, it was just beginning.

INSIGHTS

You probably guessed before Oedipus the riddles he tried to solve about the murder and himself. But the Greeks who watched the story of Oedipus on stage knew the ending, too. Their plays came from myths almost every Greek knew. For them, the point in watching the drama was to see *how* the author told the story.

Oedipus is a remarkable hero in Greek myths—mostly for what he is not. He is not the son of a god or goddess. Nor is he a man who relies on his muscles. It is through his intelligence alone that he gains power. But as his story illustrates, quick wits aren't enough. The Greeks believed no one—not even the gods—could outwit fate.

The father of psychology, Sigmund Freud, used this myth to illustrate his theory of the *Oedipus complex*. Freud thought that around the age of five, many children were attracted to their opposite-sex parent. At the same time, they felt anger toward the other parent.

Abandoning a child may seem criminal and strange to us. But it was common practice among the Greeks. Girls (because they cost money to marry off), slaves, and weaklings were among those who were deserted. But instead of taking the child to a mountain, parents usually placed the baby in a jar at a temple. There the child would be left for anyone who wanted to adopt.

The Eumenides were the goddesses from whom Oedipus sought mercy. Originally they were known as the Furies, beings who brought punishment. To constantly remind the goddesses that they should be kind, the Greeks renamed them the Eumenides. This means "the Kindly Ones."

The same root and meaning can be found in the word *euphemism*. A euphemism is a pleasant way of mentioning something unpleasant. For example, instead of saying "he died," we say "he passed away." Like the Greeks, we sometimes try to put unpleasant facts in pleasant terms.

Teiresias was an odd man, indeed. When he wasn't a woman, that is. Tciresias was changed into a woman when he hit a pair of mating snakes. Years later he struck another pair of mating snakes. That changed him back into a man.

This experience got Teiresias into more trouble. One day Hera and Zeus quarreled over who enjoyed making love more, men or women. Of course, Teiresias was called in to decide. He declared that women did.

Hera was insulted. In a fit of rage, she blinded Teiresias. Zeus, on the other hand, was pleased. So as a reward, he gave Teiresias the gift of seeing into the future.

ANTIGONE

VOCABULARY PREVIEW

Below is a list of words that appear in the story. Read the list and get to know the words before you start the story.

anarchy—lack of government; disorder
condemned—sentenced to a punishment; judged guilty
culprit—wrongdoer; lawbreaker
defiance—rebellion; refusal to give in or agree
dumb—unable or unwilling to speak; speechless
fatal—deadly
fiancee—engaged woman; bride-to-be
filtered—passed or ran through
flaws—faults
heed—pay attention to; listen to
hovering—hanging; floating
indignation—anger; resentment
inflexible—stubborn; rigid
lunged—darted or thrusted forward
prolong—lengthen; extend
prospect—possibility; chance
stench—bad odor; stink
stricken—struck
vigilant—watchful; alert
winced—drew back; flinched

ANTIGONE

from SOPHOCLES' *ANTIGONE*

Suppose that to obey one law, you had to break another one. Whom would you turn to for advice? In this story, Antigone finds out that sometimes there is no one to turn to but yourself.

Creon, King of Thebes, gazed out his palace window.[1] In the distance, just beyond the city gates, birds were circling.

"Vultures," muttered Creon. "I wondered how soon they'd come."

There were perhaps a dozen of them **hovering** overhead. They took turns diving to the ground. Creon knew they marked the place where a dead man lay unburied. Before long the sky would be full of birds. And the air would echo with the cries of hungry dogs and wolves.

[1](krē′ on) (thēbz)

Creon felt a breeze coming from where the body lay. Soon the **stench** of the rotting corpse would reach the city.

"So much the better," Creon thought aloud. "This city needs a good lesson in law and order. It will teach everyone what happens to rebels."

Creon's lesson would be one of many in Thebes' bloody history. Just the day before, a terrible war had ended. It had been fought between Thebes' two princes, Eteocles and Polynices.[2] Their father, the unfortunate King Oedipus,[3] had long ago been banished. The war had been sparked when the two princes quarreled over the throne.

The struggle seemed to end when Eteocles, the younger brother, managed to seize the throne. But then Polynices went away and organized a great army. With the help of six other generals, he tried to invade the city. The fighting was fierce and bloody. Creon's own son Menoeceus[4] died defending the city. But neither side was victorious.

At last, the two brothers decided to fight it out man to man. They agreed that the victor would be king. But neither brother lived to sit on the throne. They died at each other's hands.

Creon couldn't forget that horrible sight. The brothers lay in the dust, locked in a **fatal** embrace. How gruesome that brotherly hug had seemed!

After the death of their leader, Polynices' army fled the field. And Creon, uncle of the two princes, was named king. His first order was to give Eteocles a hero's burial. Then he gathered the citizens of Thebes together and made a speech.

"Polynices was a traitor to this city," he declared. "Therefore, he is not to be buried. He will lie where he died, food for the beasts. Anyone who seeks to cover his body, beware. To disobey this law means death!"

---

[2] (e tē' o klēz) (pol i nī' sēz)
[3] (ē'di pus or e'di pus) Oedipus had been king of Thebes. He unknowingly killed his father and married his mother. He died shortly before this story takes place.
[4] (mē nē' sūs or me nēs' sūs)

Now Creon sat in his palace watching the circling vultures. It was an ugly sight. It would get uglier still. Yet that was fitting. Polynices' rebellion had been a terrible thing. Thebes must never again experience such a war.

Little did Creon realize that his decree was soon to be disobeyed. And by his own relatives. For at that moment, his two nieces, Antigone and Ismene,[5] were meeting. They were the daughters of Oedipus and the sisters of Polynices and Eteocles.

"Ismene, come with me," requested Antigone.

"Where?" asked Ismene.

"To the plain where our brother lies unburied. No one else will cover his body and say a few prayers. So the duty falls to us."

Ismene trembled with fear. "Antigone, do you understand what you're saying?" she asked. "You heard our uncle's words. Anyone who buries Polynices is **condemned** to die."

"But think of what poor Polynices is condemned to!" said Antigone. "You know that the spirits of the unburied dead must wander the earth. Until they are buried, they cannot go to their proper rest in Hades.[6] We've put Eteocles to rest. But what about our other brother?"

"Creon declared Polynices to be a traitor," replied Ismene.

"Only the gods can decide what fate Polynices deserves," argued Antigone. "Our uncle's decree goes against the gods themselves."

"But this is too great a wrong for us to set right," protested Ismene. "Creon is too powerful."

Antigone took Ismene by the shoulders. "Ismene, listen to me! What are you afraid of? Uncle Creon's decree? When you die, you'll meet the souls of all our family. Our father, our mother, and Eteocles. And what will you say when they ask, 'Why didn't you bury your brother? Why did you leave him to suffer forever?' "

[5] (an tig' o nē) (is mē' nē)
[6] (hā' dēz) Hades was the region of the dead, ruled by the god Hades.

Antigone dropped her hands and turned away. "That **prospect** frightens me more than Creon's words. I could not face them."

Antigone turned back to her sister. "Come with me, Ismene. It's such a simple thing to do. We don't really have to bury him. We'll say a prayer and sprinkle some dirt over the body. That will be enough."

But Ismene was silent.

"Give me your answer," commanded Antigone. "Yes or no."

"No," said Ismene simply. "But I hope you succeed. I won't tell anyone what you've done."

"Oh, but I want you to!" laughed Antigone. "Tell everyone! Shout it in the streets! I'll forgive you for being timid. But I won't forgive you if you try to hide what I've done."

With those words, Antigone hurried away. Ismene sighed sadly. As always, Antigone had gotten the last word. She could be so stubborn when she got an idea in her head.

Yet this time Antigone's stubbornness could be fatal. As **inflexible** as Antigone was, their uncle was a match for her.

Antigone, however, had no second thoughts. She marched outside the city towards the place where Polynices' body rested. Close to that spot, she halted behind a large rock. From there she watched the guard who crouched beside the body.

This guard was none too happy with his job. He sat up-wind of the body. Even so, the stench was becoming unbearable. And the dead eyes of Polynices stared at him. The body seemed to beg, "Please. Bury me."

"I'll not bury you," said the guard. "I'm more afraid of the king than I am of your eyes."

The day dragged on and the guard grew weary. Try as he might, he couldn't keep his eyes open.

"Well, a little nap won't hurt," he thought. "Creon's threats will keep even the bravest folks away."

So the guard closed his weary eyes.

The guard could have sworn he slept for just a few minutes. But when he shook himself awake again, he saw a stunning change. Earth had been scattered all over Polynices' body.

In the eyes of the gods, this was enough. The guard knew it. Polynices was now as good as buried.

The guard's replacement arrived at that very moment. He, too, stared at the corpse.

"What should we do?" asked the first guard. "Should we tell the king or not?"

"*You* tell the king," grumbled the other guard. "It happened on your watch."

So the first guard slowly headed toward the palace. He stopped many times on the way. Should he really tell Creon this news? The king was known for his terrible temper.

"It might be better to leave Thebes and never come back," he muttered. But soon he found himself at the palace steps. So he summoned up his courage and went inside.

In a shaking voice, the guard told Creon what had happened. The king reacted immediately and violently.

"So you were sleeping, were you?" shouted Creon. "And you didn't even see who did it?"

"No, my lord," whispered the guard.

"Go back, then!" roared Creon. "Brush the dirt off the body. Whoever committed this crime will be back. They'll try it again. And this time, don't let them get away!"

The guard returned to his post. With the help of the second guard, the corpse was brushed clean. Then, far too frightened to sleep, they both sat watching.

Yet as **vigilant** as they were, nature stepped in. The wind rose, bringing a cloud of dust that blinded them. Then the air cleared again.

The guards blinked their eyes at what they saw. Antigone, the king's own niece, was kneeling by the body. With cupped hands, she poured dust on Polynices' chest as she whispered a prayer.

The stunned guards recovered their wits. Both leapt to

their feet and seized Antigone. This time there was no paus-
ing on the way to the palace.

The first guard entered the throne room alone. "Sire,
we've found the **culprit**," he said. "But—"

"But what?" Creon coldly demanded.

Weakly the guard gestured for the second guard to enter.
At the sight of Antigone, Creon's face turned white. He
quickly ordered the guards away. Uncle and niece stood face
to face.

"Why did you disobey my decree?" he demanded.

"Because it was wrong," replied Antigone.

"It's not your place to decide what's wrong or right."

"And is it yours?" asked Antigone.

"I am king of Thebes!" growled Creon. "Who has a
better right to decide the law?"

"The gods," Antigone answered firmly.

Creon rose to his feet. "It is my right to make laws as
I see fit."

"But not laws which insult the gods."

"Listen to me, Antigone," Creon commanded. "Law and
order are all important. They're more important than loyalty
to brother or sister, father or mother. They're even more
important than the words of the gods. And do you know
why?"

"I'm sure I don't," said Antigone.

"Because without law and order, there is **anarchy**. And
nothing is worse. With anarchy, all good things vanish. The
gods are no longer worshipped. Families turn against each
other. Obedience to the laws is the most important thing
in the world. Surely you must see what Thebes has just
suffered."

Antigone crossed her arms and refused to answer. She
simply stared at her uncle.

"You realize," added Creon, "that your punishment is
supposed to be death."

"I do," said Antigone.

"I suppose you expect me to back down."

"Why should you?" replied Antigone. "Because I'm your niece? Don't be stupid, Uncle. Punish me as you'd punish anybody else. I expect it. I'm prepared for it."

Antigone's brave words struck Creon **dumb**. His niece was more determined than he realized. His heart ached at the thought of putting her to death.

"We're a lot alike, Antigone," he said more gently. "We're both headstrong and stubborn. It's not good when two people like us cross one another. Come, let's forget all this. Obey my decree. That's all I ask."

"It's no use," said Antigone. "If you release me, I'll go straight to Polynices' body. I'll sprinkle it with dust again. The whole city will learn what I've done. There's only one way to stop me. You must kill me."

A moan startled them both. They turned and found Ismene standing in the doorway. By her face, they could tell she'd been listening for several minutes.

"Uncle," she said, stepping into the room, "how can you even think of it? She's more than just your niece. Why, she's engaged to your son, Haemon!"[7]

Ismene's words stung Creon. He didn't want to remember that Antigone was his son's **fiancee**. But whatever his relationship to Antigone, his decree had to stand.

"Antigone must die," he said firmly.

"Then you must kill me, too," said Ismene. "You see, I knew what Antigone planned. But I didn't tell you. So in my own way, I took part in her deed."

For the first time, Antigone was really angry. "No!" she shouted at her sister. "How dare you take credit for what I did! You were too cowardly to help. Now I don't need your hollow words."

Antigone turned to Creon. "I did what I did by myself. And I, alone, will die."

Creon fixed a grim look on his face and called the guards. At his orders, they took Antigone away and locked her up.

Word soon spread throughout Thebes that Antigone had

[7](hē' mon)

been sentenced to die. Yet even as the citizens spoke of her fate, Creon reviewed his decision. Could he really go through with this? It would be a terrible deed.

"I'm very fond of her," he thought. "And how can I kill my own sister's daughter? It hurts to even think of it."

Creon **winced** and wearily rubbed his hands over his face. "Yet I must remember what I told her. Law and order are more important than anything. More important than one's own flesh and blood."

Suddenly Creon felt a hand on his shoulder. He jumped and turned at the touch. The face that greeted him was even sadder than his own. Haemon had obviously heard the news.

"So it is true, father?" asked Haemon. "You mean to put Antigone to death? Don't you know that I love her? Don't you care about my feelings at all?"

Creon grasped for words. When he finally spoke, his voice was cold and hard. "My decree is final."

"Let me tell you something then," said Haemon. "For the last few hours, I've wandered the streets. I've listened to people talk—though they talk only in whispers. They say you've gone too far. They think Antigone is right. But they're afraid to tell you so."

Creon's face burned an angry red. Yet Haemon dared to continue. "Is this the kind of city you want to rule? A city full of people too scared to tell you what they think?"

"Fear is good," replied Creon. "Fear serves my purpose. If they fear me, they will obey me."

But Haemon shook his head. "That's a sad kind of obedience," he said.

Creon could no longer contain his temper. "How dare you question me!" he shouted. "When you are king, then you can decide! For now, keep your mouth shut!"

Haemon stared stonily at his father. "You may lose more than a niece," he said quietly. "You may lose a son as well." He turned and walked swiftly out of the room.

His son's **defiance** only made Creon more determined. At once he commanded his guards to drag Antigone before the Theban people. Then Creon put on his finest robe. Into the middle of a huge square he strode. And in a loud, cold voice, he declared Antigone's fate.

"Look at this woman!" he shouted. "She dared disobey a decree of your king. Not once, but twice. And when I offered to pardon her if she would keep the law, she refused."

Creon waited for the crowd to express **indignation**. But silence followed. Hastily he went on with his speech.

"For her crimes, she will be closed up in a cave near the city. She will be given enough food to last her three days."

Of course, Creon was passing a death sentence on his niece. But if she starved to death, Creon would not be guilty of her murder. At least not technically.

When Creon finished with his speech, the guards marched Antigone away. The people murmured as she passed. She looked so beautiful. She'd dressed herself like a bride, with a long, flowing scarf.

Those who were close enough saw something else about Antigone. Her eyes were filled with confusion. True, she had asked for death. Yet now death was hard to face.

Ismene followed at her side. "Sister, you did the right thing," she panted as she tried to keep up. "Forgive me for not having your courage."

"Perhaps I'm not so courageous," said Antigone. "A little while ago, I felt so different. Like a tower of strength. I'd do the will of the gods, no matter what. I believed it didn't matter whose body lay unburied. Even if it were the body of a stranger, I'd bury it."

Antigone turned puzzled eyes to Ismene. "But now— I'm not so sure. Would I do this for anybody else but Polynices? What if it were my child who lay unburied? Well, I could have another child, couldn't I? And what if it were my husband? I could marry again as well.

"But a brother or a sister is different. Our parents are both gone, and we'll have no more brothers or sisters. No, I don't think I'm so brave. I couldn't have died for anybody else. Except maybe for you, Ismene."

The gloomy cave opened before them. The sisters hastily hugged. Tears splashed from Ismene's eyes.

The guards finally separated the two women and led Antigone into the darkness. After placing a small amount of food beside her, they lit a few candles. Then they closed up the entrance with a great stone.

Alone in the cave, Antigone peered about in the dim light.

"Soon these candles will flicker and go out," she whispered to herself. "The cave will grow pitch dark. I wonder which will kill me first? Lack of air or lack of food?"

Antigone clenched her fists. "This is death already. I am dead to the world—to my uncle, my sister, my beloved Haemon.

"There is only one person I am not dead to. And that's myself. I can still see and feel. I can hear my own voice speaking."

Antigone suddenly laughed bitterly. "What foolishness to **prolong** this! How easy it is to kill this ghost I've become."

With those words, Antigone removed her scarf. She wrapped the ends around her hands and tugged.

"Yes," she whispered. "It seems strong enough."

Even as Antigone was about to end her lonely vigil, Creon received a visitor. Without waiting to be announced, Teiresias[8] strode into the throne room.

Teiresias was a blind prophet whose words were respected by every Theban. Even proud Creon rose out of respect when Teiresias entered.

"Things are not as they should be, Creon," said Teiresias abruptly. "As you know, I use birds to tell the future. I listen to their cries. But this morning, they did nothing but fight. They pecked and clawed at one another. I could make nothing out of their wild screams.

"And now I have learned the reason why. You have kept a dead man in the land of the living. You have buried a living woman, as if she were a corpse. You have mocked the

[8](ti rē′ si as)

laws of the gods. The gods are so angry, they refuse to **heed** my prayers.''

Creon swelled with anger. ''Perhaps the gods are angry at something else,'' he said. ''Perhaps they're angry that an honored prophet would take a bribe. And that's what you've done, isn't it? Those who agree with Antigone have paid you to come here. They've paid you to scare me with this talk of fighting birds.''

The servants drew back in shock, but Creon ignored them. ''Well, it won't work, old man,'' he declared. ''My first concern is the law. I must keep order in this city.''

''You forget what this city is made of,'' said Teiresias. ''It's made up of families—flesh-and-blood human beings. In your concern for laws to guide them, you've forgotten those you're guiding.''

Then Teiresias added mockingly, ''Perhaps you'd like it if there were no families. Perhaps you'd like a city made of laws and nothing else. Yes, that would be much simpler, wouldn't it? No human beings with opinions and **flaws**. Just laws—and no one to disobey them!

''Well, you may get your wish yet. Before this day ends, you will find yourself alone. The gods demand payment for the soul you've kept from them. And you will pay dearly—very dearly.'' Without waiting for a reply, the prophet left.

Creon remained standing in stunned silence. Over and over the prophet's words rang in his head.

Finally Creon nodded. ''The old man is right,'' he murmured softly. ''He's always right. There's nothing harder than admitting one's mistakes. But I must do it—and quickly.''

Creon hurried out of the palace and down to the city gates. As he walked, a crowd of Thebans gathered round him. All were curious about what their king intended.

Finally one servant darted forward. ''King Creon, may I be of help?''

''You may serve as a witness,'' Creon replied. Then turning to the crowd, he said, ''You may all serve as witnesses.

I'm going to bury Polynices. I pray it's not too late to correct the wrong I've done."

Soon Creon and his followers reached the corpse. They chased away the dogs which had nearly torn it to pieces. Creon knelt over the body and sprinkled it with dirt. Then he spoke a prayer, asking for the gods' forgiveness.

Yet Creon's gesture came too late. Even at that moment, Haemon was forcing open Antigone's tomb. He didn't know of his father's change of heart. He only hoped to set Antigone free. Then the two of them would flee Thebes and forget Creon's cruelty.

At last, the young man pushed the stone away. In the sudden gust of air, the candles inside blew out. Haemon could barely see into the darkness.

Then he dimly saw the shape of his beloved.

"Antigone!" he whispered. "Thank the gods I've reached you in time! Come with me, quickly!"

But Antigone didn't answer. Haemon reached out and touched her. Slowly she swung through the air.

With a scream, Haemon leaped back. Now he could see what hadn't been clear before. The scarf which Antigone had used to hang herself shone palely in the dark.

Haemon untied the scarf. He tenderly held Antigone in his arms and wept. Kissing her brow, he begged her to come back.

Finally the sound of voices disturbed him.

"But the tomb is already opened!" cried one.

"Then perhaps she is free already!" cried another.

Haemon turned. His father stood behind him with several followers. Creon's face was **stricken** with horror at the sight of Antigone's body. His mouth opened and he tried to speak. He wanted to beg his son's forgiveness. But no words came out.

Haemon gently placed Antigone on the ground. Then he strode up to his father and spat in Creon's face. But the insult didn't satisfy Haemon. He stepped back, drew his sword, and **lunged** at Creon. His father barely managed to step aside. Quickly guards closed in to prevent a second attempt by Haemon.

Haemon glared at his father. Then he caught sight of Antigone's body. With a howl of grief, he bent to embrace her once more. He gave her a last kiss and picked up his sword again. Before anyone could stop him, Haemon drove it deep into his own chest. He died instantly.

Creon trembled at the sight. He was too shaken to weep.

At last, he managed to speak in a hoarse whisper. "Take their bodies back to Thebes," he commanded.

Creon was not alone in his grief. His wife, Eurydice,[9] did not know of her son's death. But she had known of Haemon's plans to flee with Antigone. Her son had revealed his plans to her.

Now Eurydice sat in the palace, weeping with worry and pain. "One son dead in battle," she cried. "And the other gone forever. What greater sorrow could a mother suffer?"

Then sounds of weeping **filtered** through her own sobs. Eurydice felt chill fear at those cries. Quickly she went to the window and looked out. The sight she saw left her gasping for breath. The bodies of Antigone and Haemon were being carried to the palace. Already a huge crowd of weeping Thebans were paying their respects.

She also saw her husband, Creon, walking at their side. His head was bent, and he stumbled along like an old man.

Eurydice needed no one to tell her what had happened. The bodies told the whole story.

She sat down in icy silence, awaiting Creon. After a long time, he did appear. With swollen eyes and white face, Creon began his story. But Eurydice interrupted.

"You murdered them!" she cried. Then she picked up a dagger and held it in her shaking hands.

"I didn't wish them dead," Creon groaned.

"Death is all you think of! Death is all you make of life! And if I were dead, this would be a perfect world for you!"

"Eurydice, no!" exclaimed Creon.

---

[9] (ū rid' i sē) This is not the same Eurydice as Orpheus' wife.

"Well, I'll give you my death! And my curse as well! You've thrown away all love and friendship. May you never know such things again!"

With that, Eurydice stabbed herself. For a moment she stared at Creon, her eyes full of hate. Then she closed them and fell to the floor, dead.

Creon dropped to his knees beside her. He wept and wept—for the first time in his life. Finally he exhausted all his tears. Tenderly he picked up Eurydice's body and carried it outside the palace. There he stood in front of his people.

"Look!" he cried. "The last of my loved ones is dead! But dead as she is, she's luckier than I am. And Polynices, too, is lucky. And Antigone and Haemon, they are lucky. Soon they will join their fellow spirits in the Underworld!

"I am not so lucky, though I'm just as dead. I've taken my own life with my pride and foolishness. I have no friends, no family, no loved ones. But I must continue to walk among the living."

He set Eurydice's body down. Then he gave one last, simple command.

"Bury her," he said. "Bury all of them."

The people of Thebes did as they were told. They sang songs and prayed. They wept and shared their grief together.

Only Creon did not join the Thebans. Instead, he walked into the palace. The great doors closed behind him and he sat alone. Like a wandering spirit of the dead, he began his life of endless grief.

INSIGHTS

The playwright Sophocles wrote some of the most famous versions of the Oedipus and Antigone stories.

Sophocles was an influential author, shaping Greek drama in a number of ways. He was the first to include more than two characters on the stage. And it is said he broke an old tradition by not acting in his own plays. According to some legends, his voice was too weak.

But Sophocles certainly wasn't silent on stage. His plays speak for him, though only 7 remain out of a possible 100.

And he continued to be a powerful voice even into his old age. One legend states that his son took him to court to gain control of Sophocles' money. He said his father was too old to manage by himself.

Sophocles' response was simple: he read part of a play he was writing. The judges were more than convinced that Sophocles could still think clearly. They denied the son's charges. Then they honored Sophocles by walking him home.

According to one myth, Teiresias warned that the Thebans would be defeated in battle against Polynices' army. Only one who was descended from the Spartae could save Thebes—by allowing himself to be sacrificed. (The Spartae were men who sprang up from a dragon's teeth.)

Creon's son Menoeceus was one such descendant. To make sure Thebes was victorious, he took his own life.

continued

The Greeks had more than one reason for seeing that the dead received a proper burial. As told in the story, they thought that a corpse had to be burned or buried to prevent the soul from wandering on earth. Of course, no one wanted that to happen to a loved one.

But fear as well as love motivated the Greeks. They believed that ghosts brought disease or disaster.

In many ways, Greek burial practices were similar to our own. The dead person was washed and dressed in fine clothing. Mourners would wear black to show their grief and sometimes cut their hair. Then the body was carried through the streets as mourners trailed behind.

At the gravesite, wine was poured on the ground and animals sacrificed. This was supposed to provide the dead person with drink and food. Then after heaping flowers on the grave, the mourners went to a funeral feast.

Another custom was putting a coin in the dead person's mouth. With this coin, the soul could buy a ride into the Underworld. While this custom may seem strange to us, it was quite ordinary for the Greeks. They often carried small change in their mouths.

PERSEUS

VOCABULARY PREVIEW

Below is a list of words that appear in the story. Read the list and get to know the words before you start the story.

brooded—contemplated; thought about for a long time
castaways—shipwrecked people
confront—challenge; oppose
disagreeable—unpleasant
enclosed—imprisoned; fenced in
ghastly—frightening; horrible
gratitude—thankfulness; gratefulness
humbly—modestly; meekly
infuriated—deeply angered
intolerable—unbearable; impossible
intrepid—fearless; unafraid
loomed—appeared; came into view
lopped—chopped off
poverty—being poor; hand-to-mouth existence
relentless—cruel; without mercy
shaft—ray; beam
shuddered—shivered; trembled
tyranny—unjust use of power
vanity—too much pride; self-love
writhe—squirm; twist about

PERSEUS

Have you ever made an offer you regretted?
But pride kept you from taking back your words?
Young Perseus makes such a promise—
one that seems certain to leave him
stone-cold dead.

A cry went up among the people of the city of Argos.[1] "The king has returned!" they shouted.

At once a crowd ran out of the gates to meet the approaching chariot. The people crowded close to King Acrisius,[2] waiting for him to speak.

The king did not seem eager to talk, however. In fact, he looked impatient and tired.

"What's the news?" they asked eagerly. "What's the news from the oracle at Delphi?"[3]

"The usual meaningless riddles," grumbled Acrisius. "Not worth the journey. Now out of my way!"

---

[1] (ar' gos)
[2] (a kris' i us)
[3] (del' fi) The Delphic Oracle was a shrine sacred to Apollo, the god of light, truth, and music. A priestess there foretold the future. Throughout ancient times, the oracle was consulted by kings and leaders.

The people quickly moved aside and stared after their king. They were puzzled. The oracle had always spoken truthfully. And everyone had expected happy news. Why, then, was their king so **disagreeable**?

Alone in his palace, Acrisius **brooded**. He was not at all happy about what the oracle had said. And now he sat puzzling over what to do.

His reason for going to Delphi had been well known. Acrisius had but one child, a lovely daughter named Danaë.[4] But he needed a son to take over the throne upon his death. So he had asked the oracle if he would ever have such a son.

The priestess' answer had been anything but a riddle. "You will have no son, Acrisius," she said. The king's heart sank at this. Then the priestess added still more disturbing words. "But your daughter will give you a grandson—a fine, brave hero. And when he is grown, he will kill you."

Acrisius had **shuddered** when he heard this terrible prophecy. And now, remembering it, he shuddered again.

At that moment, Danaë approached the throne. She was, indeed, a beautiful young woman. Yet the sight of her beauty did not please Acrisius. Why couldn't she have been a son? And why was she fated to give birth to his murderer?

Danaë could read none of these thoughts in her father's face. Yet she knew something was wrong. "Father, you look so tired from your travels," she said. "Can I do anything to make you feel better?"

"Nothing," said Acrisius briefly. "Nothing for now."

Danaë nodded and quietly left the room. As the king watched her go, his anger surged. "It cannot happen! It will not happen!" he declared.

Acrisius spent the whole night thinking what to do. He was a cold and unloving man. It would have brought him no sadness to put Danaë to death. Yet he feared the gods. They harshly punished mortals who murdered their own children.

By morning the king had an idea. He summoned his

[4](da′ na ē or dan′ a ē)

metalworkers and said, "I want a house to be built. A special house. A house of solid bronze." As the workers gasped, Acrisius added, "Also, this house must be completed before the new moon rises. So begin at once."

The workers scurried to their tasks. And as the king ordered, the house was finished before the new moon rose.

Once the last bronze bit was in place, the king called for his daughter. In his coldest voice, he told her to go into the house, along with two women servants. Then he ordered the doors sealed shut behind them. Before anyone could think to protest, the deed was done.

Acrisius was still not content. He commanded that a great hole be dug. Silently the workers obeyed him.

When the hole was deep enough, the king commanded, "Now lower the house into the hole. And cover it with dirt. You will leave only one small hole over the roof."

The white-faced workers turned to stare at the king's guards. Then they again picked up their shovels.

Yet their hands sweat when they thought about what they were doing. Yes, Danaë would live. Through the little hole could come light, air, and food. Whatever else the gods might call Acrisius, he would not be a murderer. But what kind of father was he?

When the job was finished, Acrisius rubbed his hands with satisfaction. "There!" he muttered to himself. "Let's see the girl give birth to my murderer now!"

As for Danaë, she was at first terrified. Then when she saw she wasn't going to die—for food was lowered through the hole each day—she grew sad.

Finally came boredom. Weeks and months went by. There was nothing new to talk to her maids about. No new games to play.

So Danaë sat silently for hours at a time. She would stare up into the thin **shaft** of sunlight, recalling the clouds and sky. Or when it rained, she would listen to the rattle of drops on the roof. She would even try to catch the drizzle that fell through the roof hole. She liked doing that. At least it was a change.

Then just when the boredom seemed **intolerable**, something odd took place one day. As Danaë sat gazing at the sky, a chilly breeze blew into the house. Danaë shivered all over.

Suddenly the breeze was followed by a shower of gold. It flowed into the room in the middle of a sunbeam. Once inside, the golden stream twisted and turned about the house.

Though her maids drew back in fear, Danaë laughed aloud. She even reached out and tried to grab the golden shower. But it quickly moved away from her. She chased it all about the room, but couldn't catch it. Whatever it was, Danaë knew the golden shower was alive.

At last, Danaë sank tiredly into a chair. The golden shower stopped as soon as she paused. Then it crept closer until it was embracing her. The room, so chilly just a moment before, grew warm and cozy.

"Who are you?" asked Danaë dreamily. "Why don't you speak to me?"

No answer came. The golden shower hovered about her silently. Then it rolled together in a glittering ball. In a flash, it flew toward the ceiling and vanished through the roof hole.

With her strange new friend gone, Danaë sat in sadness for a moment. But somehow she knew that the golden shower would return.

And return it did, day after day. Danaë at last realized just what—or who—the golden shower was. It had to be Zeus[5] himself, king of all the gods.

Danaë had heard stories about Zeus. She knew he visited and loved mortal women in many different forms. Now she wished Zeus would appear before her in his true form. In fact, she asked him to do so many times.

But the god kept silent. He remained in his golden shower throughout all of his visits.

Whenever he left, Danaë would shrug sadly. "He has to keep up his disguise, I suppose," she'd say. "After all, I

[5](zūs)

hear that his wife, Hera,[6] is terribly jealous. She doesn't like her husband spending time with mortal women."

More weeks and months went by. Acrisius never suspected a thing. Now and again he would visit the bronze house just to see that Danaë was still there. It was on one of those visits that he heard a noise that made his heart stop. It was the sound of a baby crying.

Acrisius couldn't believe his ears. He darted to the hole and gazed down into Danaë's room. To his horror, he saw his daughter nursing a baby boy.

"Whose baby is that?" he shouted.

"Mine, of course," replied Danaë.

"A likely story! And who might the father be?"

"Zeus himself. He visits me almost every day. I've named the boy Perseus.[7] It came to me in a dream. I don't know what it means, but I think it's a nice name. What do you think of it?"

Acrisius knew very well what the name "Perseus" meant. It meant "avenger."

Acrisius realized his efforts had failed. The grandson the oracle had warned him about had been born. Still, he wasn't ready to give in to the prophecy. But how was he supposed to protect himself now?

"A son of Zeus, she tells me," thought the king. "Can it possibly be true? If it is, I can't risk putting the boy to death. The gods don't look kindly on having their children murdered by mortals."

So Acrisius came up with a different plan. He ordered the bronze house to be dug up. Then he **enclosed** Danaë and the baby Perseus in a great wooden chest. Lastly, the chest was bound shut and pushed out into the sea.

With a savage smile, Acrisius watched it float away. "Well, Zeus," he said, "it's up to you now. If the boy is really your son, come to his aid. I, for one, am through with him. But never let it be said that I killed him."

[6](hē′ ra or her′ a)
[7](per′ sūs or per′ sē us)

That knowledge would have been small comfort to Danaë. She sat huddled in the darkness, holding her son tightly. Back and forth the sea tossed them. Heavy waves lashed the chest.

Through all the confusion and terror, little Perseus never cried. He lay patiently and quietly in his mother's arms. It was as if he knew they would soon be safe.

As for Danaë, she knew no such thing. She wanted to pray to the gods for help. But she couldn't stop weeping.

"Why?" she cried. "Why has my father done this to us?"

Hours went by. The chest grew colder and colder. Danaë realized that night had finally fallen. How long the day had been! She wondered how many nights they would spend in this misery. Would they starve to death or be drowned?

At last, Danaë raised her voice in a prayer. "Lord Zeus," she cried, "you are the father of this child. Is this how you protect him? Is death all that you wish for him?"

At those words, the chest shuddered. Danaë felt as though it were being raised high in the air. Then she felt it come down again. Suddenly the chest was still.

Danaë knew they were now on dry land. But how were they to get out?

"Lord Zeus," she prayed again, "it is well and good that you've saved us from the sea. But are we to remain in this awful box forever? Send us some rescuer, please! If you won't do that, then throw us back in the sea. Let us drown and be done with it."

At that very moment, she heard a loud pounding on the box.

"Hello!" came a voice. "Is anybody in there?"

Danaë answered with a wild shriek of joy. Soon the chest was opened. Holding her baby, Danaë climbed out onto an island beach. She found herself standing face to face with a fisherman.

"Where are we?" asked Danaë.

"The island of Seriphos,"[8] explained the fisherman.

---

[8](se′ rif os or se rī′ fos)

"And I am Dictys.[9] Many fish have I caught in my day, but none quite like you."

At that Danaë managed a weak smile and even Perseus seemed to grin.

Dictys took an instant liking to the sad young girl and her baby. He took them to his house. There he and his wife soon made the **castaways** at home.

For some years, they all lived happily together. Perseus grew into a strong, healthy lad. He learned to fish from Dictys, who treated him like a son.

But happy as he was, Perseus was also restless. He had the feeling he was meant for great adventures. Much as he liked fishing, there was nothing heroic about it.

One day, Dictys' brother, Polydectes,[10] paid a visit to the household. Polydectes was the king of Seriphos. He was both wealthy and powerful. But he was no kinder or loving than Acrisius. He thought nothing of letting his brother live the life of a poor fisherman.

When Polydectes saw the beautiful Danaë, he instantly fell in love with her. He kissed her hand and said, "Come back to my palace with me. I'll make you my queen."

But Danaë politely refused. "I am already loved by the god Zeus himself," she said simply. "Surely you don't want to make the king of the gods jealous?"

After that, Polydectes came to visit almost daily. Every time he came, he asked Danaë to marry him. And every time he asked her, Danaë quietly refused.

Perseus frowned upon these constant visits. He didn't like this rude king who kept bothering his mother. But he didn't say a word for fear of embarrassing her.

One day, Perseus decided to **confront** Polydectes about the annoying visits. So he went to the palace and stood before the throne.

"King Polydectes," he said, "kindly show the manners to leave my mother alone."

[9](dik′ tis)
[10](pol i dek′ tēz)

"I don't know what you mean," protested Polydectes.

"Yes, you do," insisted Perseus. "She doesn't want to marry you. So stop bothering her."

Polydectes chuckled. "My boy, you quite misunderstood me," he said. "I didn't really mean it. I was only paying her a compliment. And I don't believe your mother took me seriously. But if it will make you happy, I'll leave her alone."

Perseus felt ashamed of himself. How could he have made such a silly mistake? He'd proven himself a terrible fool! Perseus quickly apologized, and the king accepted his apology.

But the king was lying. He had thought of nothing but Danaë day and night. And now he could see that Perseus was his enemy. The boy had to be gotten rid of.

Polydectes thought hard and fast. Then a devilish idea occurred to him. With a smile, he stood up. "Since that is settled, I'd be pleased to show you my palace. Come with me, Perseus."

So the king and young man walked through the palace halls, talking. At the end of the tour, Perseus turned to his host. "It must be wonderful to be king!" he exclaimed. "You can do whatever you want, have whatever you please."

"Ah, not everything," sighed Polydectes. "There is one treasure I've never been able to get."

"And what's that, my lord?" asked Perseus.

"The head of Medusa,"[11] said Polydectes.

Then the king told Perseus all about Medusa. She and her two sisters were known as the Gorgons.[12] Once they had been beautiful women. But their enormous **vanity** had finally angered the gods. So they were turned into horrible creatures with wings and tusks. Perhaps most **ghastly** of all, they had snakes instead of hair.

The sisters were also cursed in other ways. Whoever looked at them was immediately turned to stone. And two

[11] (me dū' sa)
[12] (gor' gonz)

of the sisters could never die. Only Medusa was mortal.

"Ah, the head of Medusa!" Polydectes exclaimed. "That would be a fine prize, indeed! Why, I could turn my enemies to stone in an instant! But it's not to be, I fear."

The king waited a moment for the words to sink in. Then he said to Perseus, "Well, you must excuse me, boy. I have many preparations to make. You see, I am getting married."

Polydectes gave a mocking smile when he saw Perseus' alarmed look. "Oh, not to your mother, of course! A bride from another island. And a good deal wealthier than your mother, if I dare say." Perseus blushed at this.

Polydectes clapped Perseus on the back. "So I really must be going. I would love to invite you to the wedding but . . . " Polydectes gave another mocking smile. "Well, most people will feel obliged to bring quite an expensive gift." He shrugged.

Perseus felt his face burning again. His **poverty** had never bothered him before. But now he saw that it kept others from viewing him as an equal. It was as though he were less than human!

Pride bubbled up in Perseus. He would bring Polydectes a gift—a gift worthy of a king.

"There is one present I can give you. Something priceless," he said. "The head of Medusa!" With that, Perseus gave a proud smile and turned away.

Polydectes grinned wickedly as he watched the young man march off. This was exactly what he'd hoped for. There was to be no wedding at all, of course. He'd made that up to trick Perseus. And the trick had worked. The foolish boy was on his way to face Medusa.

"That's the last I'll see of him!" chuckled Polydectes. "Now nothing stands between me and his mother."

Meanwhile, Perseus' pride began to cool somewhat. As it did, he saw all the problems he faced. In the first place, he didn't even know where to find Medusa, let alone how to kill her!

"Well, I can only find out by asking," Perseus finally

said to himself. So as he walked along, he stopped everyone he met. "Excuse me. Can you tell me where the Gorgon Medusa lives?"

Some people laughed. Others only stared. But no one could give him a good answer.

At last, Perseus looked up to the sky. He called out to the heavens, "Father Zeus! I've never asked you for help before, but I need it now. Please speak to me. Tell me where these Gorgons live."

A sudden motion in front of him caught Perseus' eyes. He quickly lowered his gaze and found three wonderful people standing in front of him. They seemed to have appeared out of nowhere.

One of the three was a handsome young man with a winged helmet and winged shoes. The next was a beautiful woman with gray eyes, carrying a great shield. The other was an older, bearded man. He seemed dark and threatening.

Perseus was startled out of breath. "Surely you are gods," he said at last. "Is one of you Zeus himself?"

The three gods laughed. "I'm afraid not," said the young man with the wings on his feet and head. "Zeus is busy with other matters. But I am his personal messenger, Hermes."[13]

"And I am Zeus' daughter, Athena,"[14] said the woman. "I don't bring you war, today. Just wisdom and knowledge."

"And I am Hades,"[15] said the dark man. "Zeus himself cannot come. But perhaps his brother and lord of the Underworld will do."

Perseus bowed his head low. "Indeed, I have heard of you all many times before," he said **humbly**. "But what brings you here?"

The three gods looked at one another. "You prayed for help, didn't you?" asked Hermes.

[13] (her′ mēz)
[14] (a thē′ na)
[15] (hā′ dēz)

"I did," said Perseus. "But only to learn how to find Medusa. I am young and strong and will do my best to kill her by myself. So surely I don't need three gods to tell me where she lives?"

Athena smiled and put her hand on Perseus' shoulder. "Dear boy," she said. "You can be as brave as you like. But to kill Medusa, you will have to look at her. And if you look at her, you'll turn to stone. You might find it hard to kill her then."

Perseus nodded. "As you say, goddess. But I will still find a way."

Athena smiled at his bravery. "That is what we are here for, Perseus. To help you find a way."

She removed her shield and gave it to Perseus. "Here," she said. "Take this with you. It shines like a mirror. With it you can approach Medusa by looking at her reflection."

"Then," continued Hermes, "strike her death blow with this." And he handed Perseus an excellent, sharp sword.

"It will be easier if she can't see you," added Hades, handing Perseus a cap. "If you wear this, you'll be invisible."

"But what am I to put the head in?" asked Perseus.

Athena presented him with a leather bag. "Carry it in this," she answered. "The bag will change size to fit any object, however large or small."

"I thank you all," said Perseus. "These gifts have doubtless saved my foolish life. But again, I must ask you: Where can I find Medusa and her sisters?"

"For that knowledge, you must seek out the Gray Women," replied Hermes. "They are the sisters of the Gorgons. But I warn you, they may not be eager to give directions."

"I'll make them tell me," declared Perseus. "Where do these Gray Women live?"

"Far to the west," answered Athena. "In the land of twilight."

Hermes removed his winged shoes and handed them to

Perseus. "Here," he said. "These will carry you on your way. And take my winged hat, too. You may need it as well."

Perseus thanked the gods. Then without another word, he put on the shoes and hat and flew away.

Even with Hermes' wings, it proved to be a long voyage. For days Perseus flew over land and sea.

At last, Perseus found himself in the gloomy land of twilight. The sole signs of life were leafless, twisted trees growing among knifelike rocks. Everything was a ghastly gray—the color of something not quite dead and not quite alive. Only the sigh of the tired ocean and **relentless** wind stirred the heavy air.

Perseus roamed about until he found the Gray Women huddled together. Putting on Hades' cap, he crept closer.

They were truly hideous creatures. Gray, wrinkled skin. Ugly, sharp wings. Long, skinny necks. They seemed more like vultures than women.

They were also terribly old. So old that they only had one tooth and one eye among them.

Perseus watched and listened as they chattered idly. He was shocked to see them passing the eye and tooth from one to another. Apparently they were taking turns seeing and eating.

"And now," thought Perseus, "I must convince these creatures to give me directions."

He waited for his chance. Finally the woman in the middle spoke to her righthand neighbor. "Hand me that eye," she said. "You've been hogging it long enough."

The woman on her right grumbled a little. But she removed the eye and started to hand it over. At that moment, Perseus darted forward. Then snatching the eye, he skipped back.

"What is this?" growled the woman in the middle. "I asked you for that eye. Now hand it over!"

"It's gone!" whined the woman on her right.

"What do you mean it's gone?" screeched the woman

in the middle.

"Don't tell us you dropped it!" groaned the woman on the left.

Perseus spoke up. "Don't concern yourselves," he said. "I have the eye."

"And who are you?" whined the woman in the middle.

"My name is Perseus, and I'm Zeus' son. I've come to ask where I can find your sisters, the Gorgons."

"The Gorgons!" hissed one of the women.

"Our sisters don't like company," whispered the second.

"And they'll kill us if we give you directions," squealed the third.

"Ah, I see!" said Perseus. He lightly tossed the eye up in the air and caught it as he spoke. "But I wonder if you do? Would you really rather spend your lives in darkness than give me a little information? Ah, well, if that is your decision, I'll bid you farewell."

Perseus started to walk away. But before he'd gone three steps, the women anxiously called him back. In cracking voices, they whispered where the Gorgons could be found. Then Perseus thanked them and tossed the eye in their direction. He left the three of them scrambling for it.

With Hermes' winged sandals and hat, Perseus was able to quickly reach the island where the Gorgons lived. He knew immediately he had found the place. Statues of unlucky humans stood everywhere.

At the sight of those frozen figures, Perseus shuddered. All these poor souls were victims of the Gorgons. And if he wasn't careful, he would be added to the collection.

Perseus again put on Hades' cap of invisibility. Then as quietly as possible, he crept toward the ruins of a temple. That was the place where the Gorgons lived, according to the Gray Women.

But as things turned out, Perseus didn't really need the cap. He found all the Gorgons fast asleep.

Perseus backed toward them slowly. He was careful to look at only their reflections in Athena's shield. Even the

reflections were terrible enough. Perseus could imagine how looking directly at them would turn anyone to stone.

The sister in the middle was the most horrible of them all. Perseus was sure that the one in the middle was Medusa.

Perseus inched as close as he dared. Then, gazing steadily into his shield, he raised his sword. At the last second, he breathed a prayer to Zeus. Then he swung the blade with blazing speed.

His aim was strong and true. With one blow, he **lopped** off Medusa's head.

At once Perseus snatched up the head, still without looking at it. He felt the dying snakes **writhe** in his fingers. It was a relief to drop it into Athena's leather pouch.

Perseus turned to go, eager to escape from Medusa's two sisters. But at that moment, scenting their sister's blood, they awoke.

Perseus' cap of invisibility protected him somewhat. But the sharp-nosed Gorgons could smell almost as well as they could see. In a moment, they had discovered Medusa's death. And in another moment, they smelled Perseus.

With their horrid claws, the Gorgons reached out for Perseus. One even grasped his arm. But he managed to shake her off and slip free. As fast as he could run, Perseus fled from the temple.

Yet the angry Gorgons refused to give up. Bounding from rock to rock they followed him. Only the fact that they couldn't see him allowed him to keep ahead. Yet even at that, the Gorgons came so close that he felt their breath on his neck.

Suddenly Perseus remembered his wings. With a happy cry, he leaped into the air. Behind him, he heard the roar of the defeated Gorgons.

He also heard a voice by his side. "Well done, my lad!" said the voice.

Perseus turned and looked. The god Hermes was flying beside him.

"Hermes!" exclaimed Perseus. "Where did you come from?"

"I have been with you all this time. So have Athena and Hades. I must say, you carried it off perfectly."

"Thanks to your gifts, lord," said Perseus. "Gifts which I will return to you the instant I land."

Hermes chuckled. "You'd better keep them for now," he said. "You're not quite through with your adventures yet."

Hermes vanished. But Perseus suspected that the gods were still close by. That thought comforted him on his long, lonely journey.

After flying for several days, Perseus came across a strange sight. A great giant **loomed** up in his path. As Perseus' memory stirred, he recalled tales of the Titan Atlas.[16] For his part in a war against Zeus, the Titan had been sentenced to carry the sky itself on his shoulders. Just as this giant was doing now.

Perseus spotted something else of interest. At Atlas' feet grew rich gardens and apple trees. Perseus suddenly realized he was very hungry.

"Kind Titan," said Perseus with a bow. "I have traveled long and far without food or drink. Do you mind if I have one of your apples?"

"Leave me and the apples be, little boy!" roared Atlas. "What have you done to earn them? Try bearing the weight of the entire heavens. Then you might deserve one. But not until then! Be on your way, thief!"

With these words, Atlas kicked great hills of dirt at Perseus. This made Perseus angry and he reached for his sword. Then he recalled he had a more powerful weapon.

"Gentle Titan," said Perseus, "I didn't come to steal anything. In fact, I've brought you something in return for your apples."

Perseus reached inside his bag. Looking away, he pulled out Medusa's head and showed it to Atlas. Then he returned the head to the bag and looked up.

---

[16] (tī' tan) (at' las) The Titans were an old race of gods — even older than Zeus and the other Olympians. Zeus had to fight them to gain his throne.

Even as mighty as Atlas was, Medusa's fearful eyes had worked their magic. The Titan was now a mountain of stone.

Perseus suddenly felt sorry for the Titan. "You've had to carry the sky so long," he said. "Maybe now you can rest."

Perseus again set off on his journey home. But as Hermes had said, more adventures awaited him. As Perseus flew over Ethiopia,[17] he saw another strange sight. There, chained to a rock facing the sea, stood a young woman.

Perseus flew toward the rock. He floated in front of the maiden, gazing at her. Never in his life had he seen such a sweet, lovely young woman.

In turn, the maiden stared at Perseus. Naturally she was startled to see a young man floating in the air.

"Who are you?" she asked. "Are you some god? Hermes, perhaps?"

"Neither, I'm afraid," said Perseus. "Nevertheless, I would help you if I could. So tell me, why are you chained to this rock?"

"My name is Andromeda,"[18] said the woman. "I am the princess of this land. My parents are King Cepheus and Queen Cassiopeia.[19]

"As for why I am chained here, I fear my mother's words are the cause. She dared claim that she was more beautiful than any goddess. This **infuriated** the gods. So they sent a terrible sea serpent to eat our people.

"To save the kingdom, my parents went to the oracle for advice. There they learned our kingdom could be saved— if I were sacrificed to this monster."

Andromeda's voice shook a little and she paused. Then she added, "So I wait for the serpent to come. But if you're a mortal, you'd better not. I'd hate to see you killed as well."

With these words, Andromeda lowered her head. Perseus had seen fear in her eyes. Yet he also read determination. This woman would not cry or beg.

---

[17] (ē thi ō′ pi a) Ethiopia is a country in northeastern Africa.
[18] (an drom′ e da)
[19] (sē′ fe us   or   sē′ fūs) (kas si e pē′ a   or   kas i o pē′ a)

"You're very brave in the face of death," said Perseus. "Where might I find your parents?"

"They're standing on the shore," said Andromeda. "Watching and waiting."

Without another word, Perseus flew toward Cepheus and Cassiopeia. He found them both weeping for their daughter.

"Oh, this is all my fault!" cried Cassiopeia. "This is what comes of my stupid vanity!"

"There is no need for weeping," Perseus told them. "I can save your daughter."

"I'm afraid that's impossible," said Cepheus.

"Perhaps not for me," said Perseus. "With the help of the gods, I managed to slay the Gorgon Medusa."

Hope and relief filled Cepheus' and Cassiopeia's faces.

"But tell me one thing before I kill this serpent," Perseus said. "Will you give me your daughter's hand in marriage?"

Cepheus and Cassiopeia eagerly agreed. With that, Perseus flew back to the rock where Andromeda stood. He returned just in time, for the serpent was heading straight for the cliff. The creature raised great waves as it came.

Perseus dove down upon the terrible beast. He hovered for a moment. Should he use Medusa's head again? But the young man's pride stopped him. To prove himself to Andromeda, he would fight like a true hero.

At once Perseus darted in and stabbed the serpent in the shoulder. The creature writhed at the blow and rose up. With jagged teeth, it snapped at Perseus.

But Perseus was too fast. Again and again he pierced the monster's skin.

At last, standing on a rock, he struck his final blow. The serpent gave an awful groan. Then he finally sank into the sea.

For a moment, a stunned silence followed. Then wild cheers came from people who gathered to watch.

But Perseus had ears only for Andromeda's cries of **gratitude**. Flying to her side, he sliced her chains off at once. Then he carried her back to her parents.

"I hope you haven't forgotten your promise, King Cepheus," said Perseus as he landed.

"Not at all!" said the king delightedly. "Let the wedding begin at once!"

Just then another young man rushed forward. "Andromeda!" he cried, taking the princess by the hand. "Thank the gods you are safe! Now we can be married!"

Perseus was puzzled, indeed. "Who is this fellow?" he asked Cepheus.

"His name is Phineus,"[20] said the king. "And he *was* engaged to marry my daughter."

"What do you mean by *was*?" demanded Phineus.

"If you truly loved Andromeda, you would have fought the serpent," said Cepheus. "But you left that task to this fellow here. So I'm giving her to the worthier man."

"We'll see about that!" said Phineus. And he raised his sword and rushed toward Perseus.

This time Perseus knew better than to use his sword. What would Andromeda think if she saw the man bloodily slain?

"Everybody, close your eyes!" he cried.

Everyone except Phineus did as they were told. Then shutting his own eyes, Perseus pulled the Gorgon's head out of its bag. In mid-cry, Phineus suddenly fell silent.

Perseus put the head back inside the bag and opened his eyes. Phineus, sword raised high, was now stone.

After that, the wedding went ahead smoothly. Perseus and Andromeda were married with great joy.

Afterwards, they set sail for Seriphos. Once they reached the island, they went straight to Dictys' house. There Perseus joyfully introduced his bride to his mother. But poor Danaë was too unhappy to rejoice.

Perseus, noting her sad face, quickly asked what was wrong.

"Your marriage truly pleases me," Danaë replied. "But—"

"What is it, Mother?" pressed Perseus.

[20](fin′ ē us or fi′ nūs)

"King Polydectes has threatened to kill me if I don't marry him. I scarcely know which would be worse: to be dead or to be his wife."

Perseus took his mother by the hand. "Come with me to the king's palace," he said. "However, you must promise to close your eyes when I tell you to."

"I promise," said Danaë. "But what are you going to do?"

"I'm going to give away the bride," chuckled Perseus.

With Danaë at his side, Perseus was admitted to the palace at once. In the throne room, they found Polydectes drinking and laughing with his friends.

"So," Polydectes laughed wickedly, "the **intrepid** hero returns! Your adventures proved too dangerous, I expect."

"Not at all," said Perseus simply.

"Well, why have you come?" growled the king. "Are you here again to tell me to leave your mother alone?"

"Certainly not," answered Perseus, smiling. "Marry her with my blessings! Why, I've even brought you a wedding present!"

"A wedding present?" asked the king.

"Don't you remember?" asked Perseus. "I've brought the prize you said you longed for most."

With these words, he lifted the leather bag. "Now, Mother!" he cried.

Danaë threw her arms across her eyes and Perseus tightly shut his own. Once again he lifted Medusa's head from the bag and replaced it. And once again the curse had worked. When Perseus opened his eyes, he found the king and his friends were statues.

With Polydectes dead, Dictys became king. He begged Perseus, Danaë, and Andromeda to stay in Seriphos. But the three of them decided to return to Argos. Perhaps now they could make peace with King Acrisius.

When they got there, however, the king was nowhere to be found. Perseus asked someone where Acrisius had gone.

"The people got tired of the old king's **tyranny**," came

the answer. "They drove him away. Nobody has seen him for years."

When the people heard who Perseus was, they at once begged him to take the crown. So Perseus became the king of Argos and Andromeda his queen. But before stepping to the throne, Perseus returned the gods' magical gifts. He knew that his days of adventure were over.

Life in Argos agreed with the three travelers. Yet sometimes Perseus grew bored with no serpents to fight and no Gorgons to kill. Whenever this happened, he would hold athletic contests. Often he would even join in himself.

One day, Perseus was taking part in a discus throwing contest. A crowd of people stood by watching. As Perseus swung his arm to release the discus, it slipped from his fingers. The heavy object flew into the crowd. Before anyone could even cry a warning, it struck an old man dead.

Perseus ran to the body. "What have I done!" he cried. "Who is this man?"

A hush fell over the crowd. At last, someone spoke. "Why, I recognize him! It's old King Acrisius, returned at last! But look what's become of him."

Perseus stared down at the tired, wrinkled body. "My poor grandfather!" he sighed. "But the gods must have planned this all along. From the beginning this has been your fate, old man. And mine."

INSIGHTS

What became of Medusa's head after Perseus' adventures? Most myths say that he gave it to Athena. The goddess then placed it in the middle of her battle shield for added protection.

Some myths state that both beauty and ugliness were born at Medusa's death. When Perseus cut off her head, a beautiful winged horse named Pegasus sprang from drops of her blood. In some versions, Perseus fled on this horse instead of using Hermes' wings.

Myths also add that at the time of her death, Medusa was pregnant by Poseidon (sea god). From her dead body were born the first of a long race of monsters. Among those monsters said to be related to her are

- Echidna, half-woman and half-snake
- Geryon, a three-headed monster
- Cerberus, a three-headed dog who guarded Hades
- the Hydra, a many-headed snake
- the Chimera, a fire-breathing lion
- the Sphinx, half-woman and half-lion

Perseus, on the other hand, gave birth to a much more noble family. His first son by Andromeda became the king of Persia. One of his later descendants was the hero Heracles.

Two other creations resulted from Perseus' quest. The first occurred when Perseus set down Medusa's head on some sea plants. At once the plants grew hard as rock. Thus the first coral was created.

Athena was responsible for the other creation. She was fascinated by the Gorgons' cries when they wept over Medusa's death. In trying to imitate those cries, she created a musical instrument. She called her invention the flute, or "the music of many heads."

Several of the characters from this myth have turned up in the heavens. Both Perseus and Andromeda have constellations named after them. Even the sea monster became a constellation. Look for Cetus (Greek for *sea monster*) if you want a glimpse of this beast.

Hermes, the winged messenger, is still running errands today. At least in advertising. He serves as the basis for the fast-footed messenger in FTD Florist ads.

GODS AND HEROES OF GREEK AND ROMAN MYTHOLOGY

Greek Name	Roman Name
Aphrodite	Venus
(Phoebus) Apollo	(Phoebus) Apollo
Ares	Mars, Mavors
Artemis	Diana
(Pallas) Athena	Minerva
Cronus	Saturn
Demeter	Ceres
Dionysus, Bacchus	Bacchus, Liber
Eros	Cupid
Gaea	Ge, Earth, Terra
Hades, Pluto	Pluto, Dis
Helios, Hyperion	Sol
Hephaestus	Vulcan, Mulciber
Hera	Juno
Heracles	Hercules
Hermes	Mercury
Hestia	Vesta
Odysseus	Ulysses
Persephone, Kore	Proserpina, Proserpine
Poseidon	Neptune
Rhea	Ops
Uranus	Uranus, Coelus
Zeus	Jupiter, Jove